FIREWORKS AT THE FARM ON MUDDYPUDDLE LANE

Heart-warming, uplifting romance

Etti Summers

CHAPTER ONE

Dulcie slapped her palms against the legs of her jeans to get rid of the dust on them and stood back to admire her handiwork.

The previously unkempt and uncared-for barn looked amazing, even if she did say so herself. The bales of straw that had been haphazardly thrown on one side were now stacked neatly to form pens for two goats, a donkey, a couple of Shetland ponies – all courtesy of Petra from the stables on Muddypuddle Lane – and a sheep named Flossie. Several more bales were dotted around for people to sit on, although these did have some old rugs thrown over them to make the experience more comfortable (bales of straw were **scratchy**), and there was an assortment of tables lined up against one of the walls. The tables were groaning with finger food that Otto and Walter had just brought out from the kitchen, and the appetising smell of hot chocolate and coffee hung in the air – along with the not-quite-so-enticing aroma of the animals.

Dulcie and her sister Nikki had worked hard on prettying the place up, and homemade bunting and fairy lights were strung from the beams and rafters, giving the interior of the barn a fairy grotto atmosphere.

'I think we're ready,' Dulcie announced, then cried, 'Baskets! Where are the baskets?'

Nikki said, 'You told Sammy to put them on a table near the entrance, remember?'

'So I did.' Dulcie breathed a sigh of relief. She had been so busy trying to get the farm's version of a harvest festival off the ground, that she had found herself treble checking things and often forgetting that she had already done them.

Nikki's other half, Gio, who had also been roped in to help with the event, poked his head around the open barn doors and announced, 'Your first customers have arrived.'

Dulcie panicked. 'Oh, dear, I hope they won't be disappointed. I hope we're not charging too much. What if they—?'

'Stop!' Otto commanded, leaving the food and striding over to her. He took her in his arms and kissed her on the forehead. 'It'll be fine. Take a deep breath, put a smile on your face and go say hello.'

'Okay, yeah, I can do that.' She straightened her shoulders, lifted her chin and smiled wildly.

Otto recoiled. 'Er, maybe tone the smile down a fraction?' he suggested. 'You look a little manic.'

'Sorry.' Dulcie lowered the wattage and hoped she looked more natural.

'Better.' He kissed her again, this time on the lips, then released her.

She paused for a second, drinking him in. Otto was wearing chef's whites and a cap-like covering on his head and looked as delicious as the food he had prepared. She wanted to eat him all up right now,

but she would have to wait until later.
Much later...

Pushing the wicked thoughts aside, Dulcie pulled herself together and went out into the farmyard to greet her first paying customers. They were paying to pick their own apples and pears from the laden fruit trees in the orchard. There were also a couple of plum trees dotted amongst them, and the hedgerows surrounding the orchard were full of blackthorn trees with their purple velvety sloes, as well as ripe hazelnuts, and rosehips, which could be made into the most delicious syrup, perfect for pouring over ice cream or pancakes. Otto had already prepared a large jug of it; he was hoping to persuade people to give it a go. The syrup went surprisingly well with savoury dishes, too.

Visitors could also help themselves to the sweet chestnut tree over the far side of the orchard, which was weighed down with nuts. And in one of the fields beyond lay a tumbling mass of brambles bearing loads of blackberries, which would need to be picked soon before they went to mush.

Sammy, bless him, had helped Dulcie make cardboard signs nailed to wooden stakes (Dulcie had done the nailing because she hadn't been sure that a twelve-year-old boy and a hammer were a good combination) and these directed visitors to the orchard, as well as indicating what was what, in case people were unsure about what could be picked and safely eaten. Although Dulcie was no expert, she now knew a sloe from an elderberry – which was also available to be picked.

Prior to meeting and falling in love with Otto, Dulcie would never have imagined that so many wild fruits, berries, nuts and seeds could be eaten. And flowers. Over the past few months she had eaten more blooms than the Chelsea Flower Show had on display.

There were even edible flowers to be had today, mostly in the cordials that Otto had prepared, or the ice creams he had made, such as the lavender and honey flavour, or the elderflower one, both of which were incredibly moreish.

Mind you, Dulcie thought as she strode up to the first of the farm's visitors, everything that came out of Otto's kitchen was rather moreish. As was the man himself!

'Dad, why don't you go sit in the house?' Otto suggested some time later, noticing that his father was flagging.

Even though Walter's health had improved significantly since the start of the year, when Otto had feared he might never recover from the strain of running Lilac Tree Farm singlehandedly, his dad wasn't out of the woods yet.

However, Otto had seen a significant improvement from those dark days when Walter's beloved farm had been raffled off to raise funds to cover the business's horrendous debts. And there had been even more of an improvement since his dad had been helping Dulcie get ready for the harvest festival event. In fact, it had been his father's idea.

Dulcie had been fretting about all the apples and pears that would go to waste, and Walter knew that she was also worried about the costs of keeping the farm going. So he had suggested opening the orchard up for a PYO fruit day. And things had escalated from there, culminating in Otto offering to showcase some of the recipe ideas he'd had for the cookbook he was hoping to publish, and Petra, who owned the stables on Muddypuddle Lane, offering to lend some of her animals for the children to pet and feed.

His dad had been a great help, but Otto worried that he was overdoing things.

'I'll just sit here,' Walter groaned as he lowered himself creakily onto a bale of straw. 'And maybe you could fetch me a cuppa?'

'Coming right up,' Otto said.

'Make it a proper cup of tea,' Walter called after him. 'I don't want none of those grass sweepings you're so keen on.'

Otto grinned – 'grass sweepings' was what Walter called herbal teas, and Otto had been experimenting with making teas out of the dried leaves of the various wild plants that grew around the farm and on the hillside above Muddypuddle Lane. Some of his attempts had been successful, others not so much. But that was what his cookbook was all about, helping people make the best use of their foraged ingredients.

Today would be a milestone, as he gauged what worked well and what people liked, and what they weren't so keen on. And with only a couple of dishes left to work on, he would soon be ready

to move to the next stage: finding an
agent.

Otto bustled around, in his element when
he saw the delighted expressions on
people's faces as they bit into a
chanterelle and watercress parcel made
with ground hazelnut pastry, and their
exclamations of pleasure as they had that
first taste of spinach and cobnut ravioli.
He was especially pleased at how well
the cordials and ice creams were received
by the children, whilst their parents
tucked into blueberry scones with damson
jam. He had even made a huge batch of
warming roasted beetroot and apple
soup, plus some sourdough bread to go
with it, and that was going down a storm,
because although the weather was still
fairly mild for the end of September, there
was a nip in the air and when the breeze

blew down the valley it carried a hint of the colder months to come.

Otto gazed around the barn in satisfaction. There had been a steady stream of visitors to the farm's Harvest Festival and the barn was filled with the sounds of chatting and laughter. He hoped Dulcie was pleased and that she would earn enough from this venture to keep her going for a while. Even though she still had her day job as a customer care advisor and was lucky enough to be able to work from home, Otto knew she was struggling with the costs of running the place.

Despite not having any animals to manage, apart from a growing flock of chickens, farms like this were money pits. There was always something that needed doing or paying for, and his main worry was that she would find it all a bit too much. She had worked wonders with the interior of the house, using nothing more than paint and elbow grease, but the farmhouse was nevertheless in desperate need of renovation, especially the kitchen and bathroom, and it could also do with new windows and doors, plus the chimneys would need sweeping before the winter, and he had noticed only yesterday that a tile on the roof had slipped... And that was just for starters. The outbuildings also needed attention, as did the land itself.

Yep, small farms like this ate money. But at least he could help to put something back into the coffers by providing the food and drinks today.

Not only that, he found it an absolute joy to cook for so many people again. Otto had missed this. Cooking was what he lived for and having to give up his job as Chef de Cuisine running his own kitchen in a Michelin star restaurant in London, had devastated him. But he'd had no choice; his father had needed him. And, by moving back to Picklewick and into the cottage on Muddypuddle Lane (the only part of the farm that his dad had managed to cling on to) Otto had met Dulcie, the woman he loved with all his heart.

Isn't it amazing how things work out for the best, he mused, as he handed a customer a steaming plate of ravioli. His life was perfect. Almost – and the only reason he said 'almost' was because he needed to start earning an income. All he hoped was that this foraging cookbook he was in the middle of writing would soon be published and bring in some much-needed cash, otherwise he would have to look for a job. And, as he'd already discovered, cheffing jobs around Picklewick were as scarce as the teeth in Dulcie's hens.

A day later, Dulcie put her knife and fork neatly together on the plate and leaned back in her chair. Letting out a contented sigh, she gushed, 'That was delicious.'

Otto beamed at her. 'I hoped you would say that. It's the last dish for the book.'

'It **is**? Congratulations! That's brilliant news,' Dulcie enthused, then she paused. 'What happens now?'

'I'm going to try to get an agent.' He got to his feet and began gathering up the empty plates.

Dulcie stood, too. 'Let me do that: you did all the cooking.' She cast a quick glance towards the kitchen and the mess which she knew would be in there. Otto might be a Michelin star chef, but he was sadly lacking star quality when it came to clearing up after himself.

He subsided as Dulcie waved him back into his seat, and she didn't miss the relief on his face.

She carried the stacked plates into the kitchen and grimaced when she saw the enormity of the clean-up operation. It didn't help that her kitchen had seen better days and was a far cry from the state-of-the-art, albeit tiny, kitchen in the cottage Otto shared with his father.

'Didn't Walter want to eat with us?' Dulcie called. He often did, and Dulcie enjoyed the old man's company. But she enjoyed having Otto to herself even more.

Carefully she moved a notepad and pen out of the way. The pad held Otto's scribbled notes on the dishes he had prepared this evening.

'He's gone to The Black Horse with Amos,' Otto replied. 'Darts night.'

Dulcie donned a pair of bright yellow rubber gloves and turned on the hot water tap.

Otto appeared in the doorway and propped himself up against the frame. 'He never used to play darts. I think it's an excuse to grab a pie and a pint, rather than face eating another one of my concoctions.'

'I love your concoctions. Mostly.' She thought back to the hogweed root curry he had cooked last week. It hadn't been her favourite. It hadn't been Walter's either, judging by the look on his face. However, the food Otto had made for the grandly titled Harvest Festival yesterday had gone down a storm with the visitors, as she had known it would.

To Dulcie, calling it a Harvest Festival had seemed too pretentious for what it was – a pick-your-own event with some refreshments and a couple of tame animals for the kids to pet – but everyone had seemed to enjoy themselves and she had made a few pounds. In fact, she had been shocked and delighted by the number of people who had turned up, and she vowed to do it again next year. A couple of people had asked if there would be a spring event so they could see some newborn lambs, but she would have to think about that, the issue being that she didn't have any sheep on the premises. Flossie didn't count – the ewe belonged to Walter, and neither was she in lamb.

Dulcie **had** overheard something she was keen on pursuing though, and that was the possibility of growing pumpkins for next autumn, so along with the PYO fruit, people would have the opportunity of choosing a pumpkin, and she was also toying with the idea of holding a pumpkin-carving competition.

It was all food for thought!

Speaking of food... 'How many recipes have you got now?' she asked Otto.

'One hundred and twenty-seven altogether, but if I include the variations, it's more like a hundred and thirty-nine.'

And Dulcie had eaten every single one of them. Not that she was complaining: she had thoroughly enjoyed being Otto's guinea pig, and she hadn't heard anyone else complain, either.

Except for Walter. Otto's dad might be incredibly proud of Otto's achievements, but he still preferred a traditional cottage pie and chips, and for Dulcie the highlight of any meal which Otto cooked for them was seeing Walter's perplexed expression when faced with one of Otto's more exotic dishes.

'Your dad is so much better, isn't he?' she said, plunging her hands into hot soapy water to find the pan scourer and thinking how well the elderly chap had coped with the Harvest Festival, and what a great help he had been, even if it had meant he had been exhausted for a couple of days afterwards.

When Dulcie had first met Walter, the elderly gent had been frail and shaky, incapable of looking after himself, which was why Otto had been forced to give up his job and return to Picklewick. Otto had also been faced with the awful financial mess the farm was in. He had been unaware of the situation until then, and it had been so dire that if Otto hadn't come up with the idea of the farm being raffled off, then Walter would have had to file for bankruptcy. The only part of the farm Walter still owned was the cottage halfway down Muddypuddle Lane. The rest of it belonged to Dulcie; and when she'd won the farm, she had also won Otto's heart.

Now that the money worries had been lifted from his shoulders, Walter's health, both physical and mental, had improved considerably. Otto had confided to her that at one point he had feared his father would never recover, but Dulcie was relieved that Walter was now well enough for Otto not to have to worry about him quite as much.

Otto had picked up his notepad and was currently busy reading his notes on this evening's meal. He glanced up with a smile as he placed it back on the countertop and sauntered over to her, sliding his arms around her waist and kissing the back of her neck.

'He most definitely is better, isn't he?' Otto agreed, in answer to her question.

Dulcie squirmed with pleasure, desire surging through her. She wriggled around to face him, careful to keep her sudsy gloved hands away from his shirt. 'Do you have to pick him up from the pub later?' she asked.

'No, Amos is bringing him back.'

She kissed him, then spoke into his mouth, murmuring, 'That's good.'

Amos, Petra's uncle, had just moved into his own bungalow, a converted feed shed near the stables, and Dulcie knew Amos would make sure Walter got home safe and sound.

'I thought so, too.' Otto nibbled his way from her jaw to her collarbone. 'Leave the washing up?' he suggested.

Dulcie pretended to look horrified. 'And come down to this in the morning? No, thanks.'

'Will it be quicker if I help?'

'Theoretically, yes, but only if you stop kissing me for five minutes.'

'Five minutes is too long. Three?'

'You can wait five minutes,' she replied firmly.

'I'm not sure I can.'

His lips were on her neck again, and Dulcie gasped in delight before extricating herself. 'Washing up first,' she insisted.

Otto pouted. 'Spoilsport,' he complained, but he grabbed a tea towel and began to dry. 'What you need is a dishwasher.'

'What I need is a new kitchen,' she retorted.

Despite a nice rise in her bank balance, thanks to the Harvest Festival, it would be a long while yet before she had enough funds to make that happen. Besides, there were so many other areas of the farm that needed attention, and all of them cost money.

She didn't for one second regret winning the farm, but she wished she hadn't been quite as naive. Her images of skipping through meadows with woolly lambs at her heels had been swiftly replaced by the reality of a farmhouse that was in dire need of renovation, an overgrown orchard, ambushing hens, and a sheep with a very hard head.

Thinking of hens reminded her. 'I've got to put the girls to bed before you whisk me upstairs,' she said. The 'girls' were her chickens, and they couldn't be left out all night for fear that a fox might get them.

The speed at which Otto abandoned his dish-drying duty was eye-watering. 'I'll do that,' he offered, and before she could say anything further he was stuffing his feet into a pair of wellies and hurrying out of the door.

As she finished washing the dishes, Dulcie watched him stride towards the barn and hurry inside. Two minutes later, he reappeared carrying a bucket, and she could hear him calling to the hens.

God, how she loved that man! She had lost her heart to him so completely it scared her sometimes...

But he was as much in love with her as she was with him, and he told her so several times a day. Was it too soon to take their relationship to the next level, she wondered? Now that Walter was better, there was no need for Otto to be there twenty-four-seven for his father. The old man was now more than capable of looking after himself, so maybe it was time she and Otto moved in together. Walter could remain in the cottage and Otto could move into the farmhouse with her. Otto would still be close enough to keep an eye on his dad, as the cottage was only halfway down Muddypuddle Lane, but Walter would have his independence.

And she would have Otto all to herself. The thought was a heady one.

She had just about finished tidying up the kitchen by the time he came back.

'The chickens are all safely tucked in for the night,' he announced, taking her in his arms. 'Now, where were we...?'

'You were going to carry me upstairs and make mad passionate love to me,' she reminded him.

'So I was!'

CHAPTER TWO

Otto scrubbed his face with his hand and scowled. Closing the lid of the laptop with a grunt, he flopped back on the sofa. He had spent the last few days typing up all the recipes from his scribbled notes and was now checking out the procedure for sending it to a publisher.

'What's got you all het up?' his father asked, as he put a mug of black coffee on the side table next to Otto and lowered himself slowly into the wingback chair opposite. The chair was faded and worn, bearing the scars of cat's claws, muddy paws and unidentifiable marks which were probably of spilt tea origin.

'This blasted book,' Otto muttered. 'I wish I hadn't started it.'

Walter slurped his tea and gazed at Otto over the rim of his mug.

Otto reached for his own drink, trying not to grimace when he realised his dad had made it with instant granules out of a jar, rather than attempt to use the coffee machine. Bless him, that machine baffled him, no matter how many times Otto had shown him how to use it.

'What's wrong?' Walter asked. 'I thought you had finished it?'

'I've decided which dishes to use and gathered all the recipes together, but I've yet to pitch it to an agent, and believe me, that's the hardest part. I really should have looked into the pitching side of things before I started.'

'You're going to have to explain what pitching is,' Walter said, scratching his head.

'I need an agent to get this book published, but first I've got to convince one that my idea is worth taking on. And to do that, I have to sell it to them – not sell as in money changing hands, but sell as in persuading them that the book is a commercially viable idea. Which means I must write a proposal and send them some sample recipes. That's what pitching means.' He would also have to come up with some headnotes – which were the introductions to the recipes themselves. He continued, 'Those bits I can manage, just about. It's the photography that I'm struggling with. You see, I have to send an agent some sample images as well, and I honestly didn't appreciate how difficult it would be.'

He opened the laptop again and turned it around so his dad could see the screen.

'What is it? Soup?' Walter squinted at the photo Otto had taken.

'Yes, mushroom and mugwort.'

'Hmm, I reckon I remember you making that. You served it with crackers. I forget what was in them.'

'Toasted dock seed and rye. They tasted okay, didn't they?'

Walter grudgingly admitted that they had. 'The soup was alright, too. 'I would have preferred a wholemeal loaf with it, though. Those crackers were a bit flashy, and I said at the time that I didn't think mugwort soup sounded very appealing. Anyway, the photo looks alright to me.

The soup looks like I remembered it looking.'

Otto got up and carried the laptop over to his dad, placing it on his knee. 'Here, this is what I was aiming for.' He showed Walter a professional image of a bowl of soup with some sliced mushrooms clearly visible on the top, along with a swirl of cream and a scattering of chopped parsley.

Walter examined it for a moment. 'I see what you mean.'

The mushrooms in Otto's soup had sunk and had taken most of the swirl of yoghurt with them. 'It doesn't matter what I do, I can't get my soup to look as appetising as the soup in these photos. The lighting isn't right, either.'

'You need a proper camera, not that piddly little thing on your phone.'

Otto agreed. But as well as a decent camera, he could also do with someone behind the lens who knew what they were doing. And, as he had delved deeper into what an agent would expect (he really, **really** should have looked into this beforehand, although he still would have gone ahead with the book anyway) he belatedly realised he would have to employ someone to take the photographs for him.

From what Otto could see, he had gone about it all wrong. Instead of perfecting **all** of his dishes over the last few months using Dulcie and others as tasters and then pitching to an agent, he should have sent the proposal **first**, just concentrating on a few recipes and making sure the resultant dishes were photographed to perfection.

That wasn't all; apparently he also needed the services of a food stylist, which wasn't going to be cheap. But to give his book proposal the best chance, he would have to invest in one.

Doubts rose to the surface and he wondered whether he was doing the right thing, putting all his eggs in this recipe book basket. Maybe he should knock the idea on the head and get a job as a chef? It was what he was good at, what he knew how to do. He had zero experience of publishing, and after the research he had just carried out he felt even more out of his comfort zone than he had before.

However, trying to find a job as a chef came with its own set of problems.

When he had first moved back to Picklewick, Otto hadn't entertained the idea of trying to find a job because his dad had been so ill, but when Walter had begun to improve, Otto had discovered that jobs to the level he was accustomed to working at, weren't easy to come by and would have meant a long commute – something he hadn't been prepared to do. Working long hours in a commercial kitchen was bad enough, without adding a couple of hours drive on either side, because it would have meant leaving his father alone for far too long.

Now, though, with his dad so much better, Otto no longer felt he had to be there all the time. In fact, he spent more time at Dulcie's farm than he did in the cottage on Muddypuddle Lane. More, even.

Which should have made finding a job as a head chef easier.

The problem now was Dulcie – Otto wanted to spend as much time with her as he could.

Besides, he had come this far with his recipe book, it would be a shame to give up now. He had to give it his best shot, and if that meant paying a food stylist and a photographer to show his dishes in the best possible light, then so be it.

With a sigh, he returned to the sofa and his barely-touched coffee and began to search for a food stylist.

'A food stylist? What's one of those when it's at home?' Nikki asked. She was sitting on the floor of Dulcie's living room and had been playing with the dog, a border collie puppy named Tara which belonged to her son, but she stopped and looked up at Dulcie.

'Yeah, that's what I said.' Dulcie held out her hand and the pup bounded over to lick it. Dulcie mightn't be too keen on sheep, but she was quite taken with the creature that was supposed to herd them. Tara was a real sweetie.

'I didn't know there was such a thing as a food stylist,' Nikki continued.

'Apparently they're essential in the food business if you want to advertise on telly or in a magazine. Or if you're writing a cookery book.' Dulcie giggled as the dog tried to clamber up her leg, and she slid off her chair to sit on the floor. 'Aw, she's sooo cute.'

'She's a nuisance! She ate my shoes the other day.'

'Both of them?'

'Only the one, but I can't wear them because she mangled the heel and tore the sole off the front.'

'Oh dear...' Dulcie snuggled the puppy closer. 'Were you a naughty girl for your mum?'

'Hopefully, she'll grow out of the chewing phase,' Nikki sighed.

'Apart from Tara, is everything else okay?' Dulcie wanted to know. She knew Nikki was concerned about Sammy starting a new school and he seemed to be settling, but she wanted to make sure as she hadn't managed to check in with her the other day.

Her sister grinned. 'Things couldn't be better, both for me and for Sammy.'

Dulcie glanced toward the kitchen and the door to the rear of the farmhouse. Sammy was outside checking on the chickens, Kevin in particular. Kevin was his own hen and was a female, despite her name. 'How has he been in school?' she asked.

Sammy was the main reason that Nikki had moved to Picklewick. Having been badly bullied in his former school, Nikki had brought him to the village at the beginning of September to make a fresh start. That she had fallen in love with a local policeman over the summer had also been a deciding factor.

'He's still loving his new school,' Nikki assured her.

Dulcie asked, 'Are you still loving yours?'

Nikki was a teacher and she had also started a permanent job in a new school, having been a supply teacher for years in Birmingham. 'It's fab. I'm working with a great bunch of people and the kids are lovely, too. Anyway, back to Otto's food stylist; what do they do exactly?'

'Make food look better than it does in real life,' Dulcie replied. 'And you wouldn't believe some of the things they get up to.'

'Such as?'

'You know when you see a lovely bowl of fresh fruit in an advert? Did you know that they use hairspray to make it look all shiny? And if you see water droplets on, say, an apple – that could very well be glycerine mixed with water and sprayed on.'

'No!'

'Uh-huh. But that's not all. Imagine seeing an advert for a roast chicken, fresh out of the oven; it's probably raw chicken that has been blasted with a blow torch to brown and crisp up the skin, then coated with shoe polish mixed with soy sauce to make it look cooked and juicy. Oh, and you know how a whole chicken can deflate when you take it out of the oven...? Shove a balloon inside it and blow it up. It makes the bird look really plump.'

'Well, I never! And Otto is going to employ someone to do that for him?'

'Yep, and a photographer.'

Nikki whistled. 'I bet that's not cheap.'

'I doubt it is.' Dulcie pulled a face and her gaze dropped to the pup in her arms. It wasn't the **cost** that was worrying her.

'What aren't you telling me?' Nikki asked.

Dulcie glowered. 'You and your spidey senses.'

'It comes from working with kids for years. My spidey senses are honed to perfection. Now, spill.'

'Otto has found a stylist. And a photographer. In London.'

'So?'

Dulcie wondered how to phrase her concerns without sounding totally pathetic. 'I'm scared he won't come back,' she finally admitted in a small voice.

Nikki burst out laughing. 'Of course he'll come back! Picklewick is his home. His dad is here – and so are you.'

'He lived in London for years, and he only came back because Walter was so ill.' She swallowed. 'But Walter is so much better now, and I know Otto misses running a kitchen. What if he realises just **how much** he misses it? What if I'm not enough to make him want to stay in Picklewick?'

'Has he said anything to that effect?'

'No, but...'

'Does he love you?'

'Yes, but...'

'There you go! You've got nothing to worry about. Now, are you going to put the kettle on, or do I have to die of thirst?'

Dulcie handed her sister the sleepy pup and scrambled to her feet, still not convinced. Even though Otto never went a day without telling her he loved her, she couldn't say why but she had a feeling that she mightn't be enough for him, and she was dreading his impending trip to London.

'Are you sure this will work?' Dulcie asked Otto as they walked down the lane. He took her hand in his and gave it a squeeze.

She was looking doubtful, but Otto knew what he was doing. As did Petra, who had suggested the arrangement in the first place.

It had all come about because Walter had thought Flossie was lonely and had said as much to Amos, who, in turn, had mentioned it to Petra. Petra had pointed out that Lilac Tree Farm had more grazing than it knew what to do with, and that it might be a good idea to put Flossie in one of Dulcie's fields so the goats could keep her company. No doubt Flossie would prefer to be with other sheep, but considering Walter didn't own any others, goats were better than nothing.

Otto smirked to himself as he remembered the first time Dulcie had met Flossie – and Dulcie's reaction to the sheep. Dulcie had been petrified, locking herself in the farmhouse, convinced the ewe had been trying to attack her, when all Flossie had wanted was a cuddle. That was the problem with hand-raising lambs, they became entitled, and Flossie had very definite views of what she liked, and that consisted of being inside the house and being fussed over. Which had been cute when she was tiny, but not so cute now she weighed about sixty kilos.

Dulcie narrowed her eyes at him. 'What are you smiling about? Don't you think I can handle a goat?'

He and Dulcie were collecting the animals from the stables to bring them up to the farm. Nathan, the stable's manager, had put them in the barn ready, and that was where they were heading now.

Otto sniffed the air, noting the familiar and rather pleasant aroma of horse. He had grown up with the whiff of sheep and horses, and he knew which he preferred! Horses smelled considerably nicer: in close confines or in large numbers the aroma of sheep could be overpowering.

The stable yard was empty, but Otto knew his way around and he led Dulcie to the large neat barn that held most of the hay, straw and feed that would see Petra's horses through the winter. It was currently full of bales, but there was a space near the huge metal doors that had been made into a pen, and this was where Princess and her daughter Toffee were held. Both goats were wearing halters, and Princess bleated a greeting.

Dulcie reached into the pen to scratch the goat's head, and Otto marvelled at how far Dulcie had come since she had won the farm. Not so long ago, she would have run screaming if a goat tried to eat her sleeve, but all she did now was push the animal away.

'If you're going to be antisocial, don't expect to be petted,' she scolded the goat, who gave her a devil-eyed stare and tried to butt her. 'You can cut that out, too,' Dulcie added. 'If you aren't going to be nice, you won't get to eat all that lovely grass in my field.'

Otto saw her flinch when she realised what she'd said, and he draped an arm around her shoulders to show that he wasn't bothered. Anyway, it **was** Dulcie's field: she had won it fair and square along with the rest of the farm. He knew she still felt awkward about it, but he wished she didn't. He didn't want her worrying that she might say the wrong thing, so he gave her a kiss on the head and said, 'You don't have to feel bad about it.'

'I know, but I can't help it. The farm has been in your family for generations.'

'But look how much better my dad is. I'd prefer him healthy, happy and farmless, rather than stressed, ill and still trying to run it. Or worse,' he added darkly.

'Would you have kept it on if... you know...?' Dulcie asked.

'If something had happened to Dad? Not a chance.' Otto might have been brought up on a farm, but farming wasn't in his blood. He had wanted to cook.

Otto blamed his mum for that. She had tended the farm's veggie plot and had delighted in making tasty and nutritious meals from what she grew. And just as his father had expected him to help on the farm, she had expected him to help around the house. Otto had quickly concluded that he preferred cooking to sorting the laundry, so that was what he had concentrated on. After his mother died when he had been in his mid-teens, Otto had taken over the role of cook and

his love affair with creating glorious
dishes had begun.

Catering college had been followed by the
offer of a job in Thornbury, and from
there he had moved to London, and his
rise up the ranks in the kitchen had been
steady, until he was made Chef de
Cuisine shortly after his thirty-first
birthday.

Three years later, he had received a
phone call from Amos telling him that his
father had collapsed.

The loud ring of his mobile dragged Otto
out of his reverie, making him jump, and
he scrambled to answer it, smiling when
he recognised the number.

'Remi, my man! How the devil are you?'
he cried, hooking a lead rope off a peg
near the door and throwing it to Dulcie.

She caught it deftly.

Otto put his hand over the phone and said to her, 'I'll catch up with you in a minute.' He turned away, hoping his old mate had some good news for him.

'Pretty damned good.' Remi's usually faint French accent seemed more pronounced, or did it appear that way because Otto hadn't spoken to him in ages. 'I got your message – of course you can stay with me. I'll book some time off work; they owe me days and days of holiday.'

Otto guessed the reason why Remi had so many holidays to take. Remi had probably thrown himself into work after his relationship with his girlfriend had broken down. 'Sorry to hear about Steff, man.'

'Eh, it's water under the bridge. Last year's news. Now, where shall we go? Pascal Ferkin – remember him? – he has opened his own restaurant. I've heard it's good. Or do you want to go to The Fern?'

Otto pulled a face and said, 'Not really. Maybe another time.'

'Okay, you decide.'

'Let's try Pascal's place.'

'Bien. I'll book a table. When are you coming to London?'

'Next Tuesday.'

'It'll be good to see you, my friend.'

'You, too.'

Otto was still grinning when he caught up with Dulcie, who was halfway up the lane, a lead rope in each hand, attached to a goat.

She thrust one of the ropes at him as she dragged Princess's head out of the hedge. The goat's face emerged, leaves poking out of the side of her mouth as she chewed.

Otto explained, 'That was Remi. He said I can stay with him. I didn't fancy being in a hotel. After living in London for so long, I would feel like a tourist if I had to book a room.'

Dulcie gave him a sharp look but didn't say anything.

He carried on, wondering what he had said or done to warrant it. 'It's such a shame about him and Steff. I could have sworn they were a match made in heaven. I wonder why they split up?'

'You can ask him when you see him,' Dulcie suggested, panting ever so slightly as they climbed the hill.

Otto was horrified. 'I'm not asking him that! If he wants to tell me, he will. But I suspect we'll just talk shop or chat about sport.'

'You are such a bloke!' Dulcie cried with a roll of her eyes. 'It **is** okay for a fella to show his feelings or to give a mate a cuddle, you know.'

They had reached the field which was going to be the goats' home for the foreseeable future, and Otto opened the gate. 'Nope. Not going to happen. I'm saving all my cuddles for you.'

He removed the halters and set the goats free. Princess was off like a shot, eager to say hello to Flossie, who had been nibbling at the grass over the far side, but who was now hastily trotting towards the new arrivals and loudly bleating a greeting.

'I like cuddles,' Dulcie told him, snuggling into his side and wrapping her arms around his waist.

Otto liked cuddles, too. He liked kisses even more, and he took the opportunity to lower his mouth to hers.

'I wish you were coming with me,' he murmured when they paused for breath.

'So do I, but as you pointed out, you'll be busy preparing your dishes – or rather, the food stylist will. Isn't it mad that such a thing exists! Anyway, I've got livestock to care for.'

'Listen to you – **livestock**. You sound like a proper farmer.'

Dulcie turned to look at the field where the goats and sheep had settled down to graze. 'I feel like one,' she said. 'I really love it here.'

'And I love **you**,' Otto said, emotion making his voice hoarse. He loved this woman so darned much!

He was going to miss her when he was away – but at least it would only be for a few days. Who knew that it would take falling in love with Dulcie to make him look forward to returning to Muddypuddle Lane?

Dulcie wound the curly cord of the 'so-old-fashioned-it-was-retro' phone around her finger later that evening, and confessed to her friend just how much she was going to miss Otto.

'Aw, it must be love,' Carla said.

Dulcie could hear the clatter of plates and hoped she wasn't interrupting Carla's meal. 'It is,' she sighed. 'Look, I can tell that you're busy—'

'Not too busy to hear all the goss from my favourite best friend.'

'I thought I was your only best friend,' Dulcie whined.

'You are. More or less. But since you decided to bugger off and live in the wilderness, I've had to bump Vicky up a notch.'

'Vicky?' Dulcie felt quite put out and rather sad.

'I love her to bits, but she'll never replace you,' Carla soothed. 'Now, back to Otto. Is he going to London to speak to a publisher?'

'I wish! That's the step after the next one. He's got to get a proposal together first, which is why he's going to London next week so the dishes can be photographed to perfection, then he has to send the proposal to an agent or two, and if an agent takes him on, they try to sell his idea to a publisher.'

'Blinkin' heck, that's a bit involved, isn't it?'

Dulcie let out another heartfelt sigh. 'You can say that again. One minute he's all fired up about it, the next he's in the doldrums because it's becoming too much. He hasn't said anything to me, but

I sometimes get the impression he wishes he hadn't started it.'

'What would he do instead? Look for a job?'

'He'll have to, I suppose.'

'You sound down in the dumps yourself,' Carla observed. 'I tell you what – how about I come for a visit? I haven't seen you since you left Birmingham.'

Dulcie had been living in Picklewick for almost six months and Carly had yet to see the farm. In the beginning Dulcie hadn't wanted anyone to visit because of the state it was in – although she had welcomed Nikki's help when she understood just how much renovation it needed. Then, later in the summer, when she deemed that the farmhouse was respectable enough to receive visitors,

Carla hadn't been able to make it for one reason or another.

'That would be fab!' Dulcie cried.

She now had something to look forward to when Otto was away, and hopefully a visit from her effervescent, irascible friend would help take her mind off him – because even though he would be gone for only a few days, she was going to miss him like crazy.

CHAPTER THREE

Dulcie called to the two goats and the sheep, as she leant on the top of the gate and rattled a bucket of pellets. As soon as the animals began to run towards her, she upended the bucket and scattered the contents in a line, so all three animals had access to the food.

Petra had suggested giving the goats supplementary feed because she was thinking about breeding from Princess again this year, and she wanted her to be in the best possible condition beforehand. Toffee was too young. To Dulcie's untrained eye, although the goat looked old enough to be bred from, apparently she was still only a youngster.

It would be nice to have a baby goat around next spring, Dulcie mused as she stroked Princess's soft ears. She liked goats better than sheep, she decided, and was more than happy for this pair to remain on the farm for a while.

With those animals fed, it was time to call the chickens in for the night. They had their own little house in the orchard where they spent their days scratching around for grubs, insects and tasty green leaves, and their nights safely tucked inside the coop. Each morning she would let them out and gather the eggs they had laid, and she often had one for her breakfast.

Dulcie lingered over the task, in no rush to go inside. Otto had only left for London this morning, but she was already feeling his absence keenly. Even though he didn't spend all day, every day at the farm, knowing he was a mere short stroll away made all the difference.

She had promised him she would look in on Walter, and although it might be a bit soon (Walter would be fine on his own for tonight) she decided to take a walk down the lane and call on him anyway. It would be for her benefit just as much as his, and they would be able to keep each other company for an hour or so.

Actually, she thought, as she dawdled down the pitted, potholed track, he probably felt less lonely than she did because he had Peg for company. Walter doted on the former sheepdog. Otto had told her that when he had first returned to Picklewick, his dad had point blank refused to move into the village's lovely care home or into an assisted-living flat because he would have been unable to take his dog with him. Which was the reason why Otto had been forced to move back to Picklewick permanently.

'Dulcie! I was just thinking about you,' Walter announced when he opened the door and saw her standing on the path. 'I keep telling you, there's no need to knock. Come in.' He waved her inside and Dulcie gave him a peck on the cheek. 'Tea? Or something stronger?' he offered.

'Tea, please,' she said, but quickly changed her mind on seeing his crestfallen expression. 'On second thoughts, I'll join you in a small one.'

Walter's 'small one' turned out to be a large plum brandy, which she sipped at cautiously. Surprised to discover that it was delicious, although rather strong, she took another, larger mouthful. It trailed a warm path from her throat to her tummy, and she cautioned herself not to drink too much. Carla was arriving tomorrow and no doubt they would indulge in a bottle of wine or two, so the last thing Dulcie needed was to start the morning off with a hangover.

Like Carla, Dulcie had taken a couple of days off work and she was looking forward to it immensely. It would be great to have a proper girly natter: phone calls just weren't the same.

'Have you heard from Otto?' Walter asked, after he had lowered himself carefully into his chair. He dipped his little finger into his glass and offered it to Peg.

'Erm, are dogs supposed to drink brandy?' Dulcie raised her eyebrows.

'No, but she likes to taste whatever I'm having, and she'll keep pestering me until I give her some. See, she's not keen.'

The dog had sniffed his finger, then backed away, not liking the smell.

'Otto has arrived safely,' she said, answering Walter's question. Otto had messaged her as soon as he had parked the car, and she had imagined him unloading all the foodstuff he had taken with him ready for the shoot tomorrow.

Shoot...? She sounded as though she knew what she was talking about, when in reality she didn't have a clue. All she hoped was that it went well, and that Otto was happy with the results.

Suddenly the book seemed very real indeed. Up until this point, for Dulcie it had been a bit pie-in-the-sky, but now that he was actually in London and meeting with the food stylist and the photographer, she began to hope Otto might find a publisher. If he did, it would stop him fretting as much. He tried to hide it from her, but she knew he was concerned about finding a job. Now that he was in a position to go back to work, he was desperate to start earning again. Walter's pension only went so far, and although she knew that Otto had some savings, they were dwindling rapidly.

As though he had read her mind, Walter said, 'He needs to get himself a job. It's all well and good trying to write this recipe book of his, but what if it doesn't sell? And what will he do after it's published?'

'Write another?'

Walter harrumphed. 'I suppose, but from what I've read in the papers there's no money in it. If his mother was still alive, she'd tell him straight, but he doesn't listen to me. He never did.'

'Was he a wilful child?' Dulcie asked. She had gleaned snippets here and there about Otto's childhood, but those had been from Otto himself. It would be interesting to get Walter's take on it.

'Woefully,' Walter said. 'I wanted him to stay here and farm with me, but he was having none of it. All he ever wanted to do was cook.' He examined the contents of his glass for a while, then looked at her, and Dulcie saw the pride shining out of his eyes and heard it in his voice when he said, 'My boy has done well for himself.'

'He has,' she agreed.

'It's good that he didn't listen to me. Not everyone is cut out for this life. Don't get me wrong, he would have made a decent enough farmer, but his heart wasn't in it. I used to think it a shame that he would have sold the farm after I passed. But you're here now, and I can rest easy knowing it's in good hands.'

Dulcie wasn't sure about that. She didn't know the first thing about farming, and she wasn't sure she wanted to. According to Otto, her farm was only suited to sheep and that was mostly due to being able to graze them on the common land on the hills above. Cattle didn't do so well up there, apparently: which wasn't an issue, considering she didn't intend keeping cattle. Neither did she intend to keep sheep. She would just have to come up with some other ideas of what to do with her land.

Walter was saying, 'My brother never wanted anything to do with the farm, either. He buggered off to Australia thirty-odd years ago.'

'I didn't know Otto had an uncle in Australia; he never said.'

'Probably because he never met him, and I hardly talked about him. We got a Christmas card every year, but that was about it. Anyway, Emrys is dead now – he passed away last year.' Walter looked wistful. 'I wish I could have seen him one last time.'

He fell silent and Dulcie concentrated on her drink. The clock on the mantelpiece ticked loudly and Peg whimpered once, her paws twitching as she dreamt.

Eventually Dulcie said, 'Do you regret staying on the farm? Did you ever want to do something else, or move away?'

Walter shook his head. 'Farming is all I ever knew. I was the eldest, so I took over the farm from my father, and it was no surprise Emrys wanted to do something else. I didn't expect him to emigrate, though. Still, from what I can gather he had a good life. He got married and had kids, so I've got a sister-in-law out there and a couple of nieces. I can't even remember their names.' He made to get up. 'It's on the Christmas cards he used to send. I kept a couple.'

'Show me another time,' she suggested, noticing how tired he looked, and he sank back down. 'I'd better be off. Can I get you anything before I go?'

'No thanks, love. I'm good. Take care going up that lane.'

'I will,' she promised, and she kissed the top of his head as she left.

As she made her slow way up the hill, Dulcie thought how very different Otto's life would have been had he stayed on the farm, and how it wasn't always easy to escape one's roots. Fate had brought Otto back to the farm on Muddypuddle Lane, and fate could just as easily take him away again. She simply couldn't shake the worry that he might be seduced back to the capital and his old life.

Otto gazed around the restaurant with a critical eye, noting what was working well and what he would change if the place was his.

Pascal had done a good job. The interior was slick and chic, and the vibe was intimate but also industrial – almost as though diners were eating in a friend's converted warehouse apartment rather than a restaurant, and that was what made it trendy. Other people obviously thought so too, because the place was busy.

But no matter how good the vibe, the only thing that truly mattered was the food. And so far, Otto was impressed. Pascal's menu was crisp and en pointe, and the first course had been a wonderful blend of flavours and textures, as well as being presented perfectly. Thus far, he couldn't fault it.

'Pascal is giving The Fern a run for its money,' Remi observed, his fingers curled around the stem of a glass of chilled

Vouvray. The open bottle sat between them on the table, and Otto took a sip of his and swilled it around his mouth. The wine was deliciously dry.

'How is Alistair taking it?' Otto asked.

Remi snorted. 'He's threatening to sack his head chef.' His response was as dry as the wine they were drinking.

'That sounds like him,' Otto acknowledged.

'The place isn't the same without you. It only won its Michelin star because of **your** food.'

Otto felt bad. But he hadn't had any choice other than to leave. His father's health was more important than a job: no matter how much Otto had loved it.

However, he had no illusions that he was indispensable. The Fern would be okay. Alistair just didn't like change, that was all. But restaurants had to be flexible and quick to respond to the ever-changing tastes of the public, and Otto's forte was that he had been particularly effective at persuading Alistair to put new dishes on the menu.

'How about you?' he asked, keen to change the subject. He didn't want to dwell on the fortunes of his former boss, because it made him feel he should be doing something to rectify the situation.

'Eh, you know, **comme ci, comme ça**.' Remi held out his hand and rocked it from side-to-side. 'I'll get over Steff soon enough.'

Otto was reluctant to ask, but he remembered what Dulcie had said, so he asked anyway. 'What went wrong?'

'Work.' Remi's reply was short. Then he did a one-shoulder shrug and added, 'You know how it is. We chefs work in the evening and at weekends, all the time. It didn't sit well with her.'

'She knew what you did for a living before she moved in with you,' Otto pointed out.

'Maybe she was hoping it would change.'

'As in, you going to work in an office or something?'

'Perhaps.'

'I can't see you sitting behind a desk all day.'

'I can't see you milking cows all day.'

Otto barked out a laugh. 'Dad farmed sheep, not cattle. And he no longer owns the farm, remember?'

'Ah, yes... The delectable Dulcie owns it now. How goes it with you two?'

Otto couldn't prevent a beaming grin from spreading across his face. 'It's good.' He had told Remi all about Dulcie.

'I think it is more than good,' Remi replied, astutely. 'I would like to meet the woman who is keeping you away from London.' Otto opened his mouth to object, but Remi leapt in. 'Your father is well again, no? So there must be another reason you are hiding away in the countryside – and I believe **she** is it.'

'I'm not hiding,' Otto objected. 'And my father isn't back to full health yet.'

'When he is, will you come back?'

'No.'

'Then I am right.' Remi looked very satisfied with himself.

'It's early days yet.'

'But you are in love: I can tell.'

'I might be.' Otto studied his wine glass, wishing the service was quicker so that the main course would appear and put an end to this conversation. His face was growing warm, and he berated himself for going down the relationship rabbit hole in the first place.

Remi laughed. 'You had better not forget to invite me to your wedding.'

'Hang on – who said anything about a wedding?'

His friend sent him a knowing look, then Remi's expression became serious. 'Joking aside, what will you do with yourself? Please say you will continue to cook,' he begged.

'We'll see. I've got to get this book out of the way first, before I look for a new position. And I'm not sure I want to go back to those long and unsociable hours.'

'You are thinking of me and Steff?'

Otto was, but he had already been thinking about the strain that working in a restaurant kitchen would put on his relationship with Dulcie. But what else was he to do? Giving up being a chef meant that he was giving up a massive part of himself. He had sacrificed a great deal to get to where he was before his father became ill, and he knew how disappointed his dad had been when Otto had made it clear he didn't want to run the farm. Had that been all in vain?

It was this fear that had driven him to think of his recipe book for foraged ingredients in the first place, hoping it would bring in enough income to tide him over until his dad could cope on his own. After which, Otto could either find a chef's position that he could commute to from Muddypuddle Lane, or (and he had secretly been harbouring this hope) he could return to London.

Then he had fallen in love... and he was back to square one as far as his career was concerned.

Let's just hope this cookbook pans out, he prayed.

CHAPTER FOUR

'Oh. My. God!! You didn't tell me Picklewick was so cu-ute!' Carla cried as Dulcie drove through the village the following afternoon.

'I did. You probably weren't listening.' Dulcie had picked Carla up from the railway station in Thornbury and they were now heading towards Muddypuddle Lane.

'Bet there's not much nightlife, though,' Carla continued, her head swivelling from side-to-side as the car negotiated the bustling main street with its quaint artisan shops. There wasn't a single high-

street chain in the village, which Dulcie
found quite amazing and very charming.

'Not a lot,' Dulcie agreed, waving to Gio,
who was leaning against his police car, a
refillable coffee mug in his hand. He was
parked outside his favourite cafe.

Carla's eyes were out on stalks. 'Wow!
That copper is hot!'

'That copper is Nikki's partner,' Dulcie
informed her with a smile.

Carla muttered, 'Lucky cow. I knew I
should have insisted that you invite me
first.'

'Even before my own sister?'

'Yep.' Carla nodded confidently. 'I could
have got to him before she did.'

'Oh no, lady, you're not getting up to your old tricks in Picklewick. I've got to live here, remember?'

'What tricks?' Carla's expression was one of total innocence.

'Your love them and leave them tricks. You've had more boyfriends than I've had hot dinners.'

'You sound like my mum.'

Dulcie shot her a look. 'Don't you dare imply I'm getting all mumsy.'

'If the hat fits...' Carla teased. 'Look at you – all you need is dungarees, wellies and a flat cap.'

'That's not mumsy, that's more Farmer Giles.' Dulcie suddenly giggled. 'It's so good to have you here. I've missed you.'

'I've missed you, too. Why did you have to win a farm in the middle of nowhere? Why couldn't you have won a villa in Italy or a swish apartment in London? That would have been far more fun.'

When Dulcie had first set foot on the farm she might have agreed with Carla. But not now. Dulcie had fallen in love with the house, the village and Otto, and she couldn't imagine living anywhere else. The thought of going back to her old life in Birmingham and that pokey flat she used to rent, made her shudder. It was alright for Carla – although she was still living at home her mother was away so much with work that it felt as though Carla had her own place. And when her mum was actually there, they were like ships passing in the night. Carla's mum just let her get on with it, whereas if Dulcie were still living at home Dulcie's mum would have been in her face all the time, so she had moved out as soon as she could afford it. Unfortunately, the only flat she could afford hadn't been the best.

'If I hadn't won the farm I wouldn't have met Otto,' Dulcie pointed out as she turned the car into Muddypuddle Lane, and it bounced and juddered up the track.

'Dear god, let me out – I'll walk from here,' Carla complained. 'My teeth are rattling.'

'You get used to it.'

Carla gazed around. 'You really are out in the sticks. There are horses in those fields.'

Dulcie chuckled. 'I know. Would you like to have a go on one?'

'Me, on a horse? I don't bleedin' think so!' Her friend shuddered. 'They're huge.'

'Petra has smaller ones. Look, this is where my land starts.'

Her eyes wide, Carla let out a gasp. 'You own all this?'

'Yep.'

'I know I've seen photos, but they don't do it justice. Is that your farmhouse? It's gorgeous!'

They had just turned into the farmyard and Carla was already reaching for the door handle. 'You lucky cow. You lucky, lucky, lucky—'

'Cow? I know.' Dulcie got out. 'You would hate it though. As you said, it's in the sticks.'

'I think I could get used to it, if it means owning a house like this.'

'It's quite old-fashioned inside, remember?' Dulcie warned her, dragging Carla's overnight bag from the back seat.

'I don't care,' her friend said, but when Dulcie pushed open the front door and showed her inside, Carla's face fell.

Dulcie had been hoping for a more enthusiastic reaction, considering all the decorating she had done over the summer, but she knew the farmhouse was what influencers would call 'rustic'. It might look great on Instagram, but the reality was slightly different. The old, patterned carpet was still on the stairs because she couldn't afford to replace it yet, and the bannister had a couple of spindles missing. The original flagstone floor in the hall was a nice feature though: Dulcie had cleaned the tiles and resealed them and they looked as good as new. And although the walls would benefit from being replastered, they had been painted a light sunny yellow and she had hung some prints to brighten it up. All in all, she didn't think it looked too shabby, so Carla's reaction was rather disappointing.

'I don't think it's old-fashioned,' Carla said, her gaze darting to and fro. 'I think it's quaint. Please don't tell me you've stripped out all the period features.'

'You like it?' Dulcie asked uncertainly.

'I do! You lucky, lucky...'

'Come and see the rest of it, then I'll introduce you to my chickens. We've got goats too, but they're not mine, they're

Petra's. They're only here to keep Flossie the sheep company.'

'I'd rather not, if you don't mind.'

'Chicken,' Dulcie teased. 'See what I did there?'

Carla clucked her agreement, and Dulcie let the matter drop. She had felt exactly the same way about the feathery creatures when she had first set foot on the farm, but she was quite attached to them now, and the goats had also grown on her. She rather looked forward to greeting them every morning. She still wasn't keen on Flossie, though.

'Drink?' she offered. 'I've got wine, unless you think it's too early.'

'It's never too early for wine,' Carla enthused.

Dulcie showed her to one of the guest bedrooms, the one with the nicest view over the valley, and left her friend to freshen up whilst she got the bottle out of the fridge and poured them a glass each.

'It's a pity it's too cold to sit outside,' Dulcie said, as they took their drinks into the sitting room. 'One day I'd like to put French doors in here, or full-length windows to make the most of the view.'

'That's a great idea. I wonder what it'll be like here in the winter. Do you think you'll be snowed in?'

'It's a possibility. But the village is within walking distance, so I should imagine we'll be fine.'

'We? As in... you and Otto? I wish he was here so I could meet him. Can I be a bridesmaid?'

'Gosh, it's a bit soon to be thinking about weddings,' Dulcie said, a blush spreading up her neck and into her face which had nothing to do with the temperature in the room, considering she hadn't lit the fire yet.

'But if he asked, would you say yes?'

'I might.'

Carla studied her. 'You deffo would,' she declared. 'Would you sell this place?'

Dulcie pulled a face. 'Did you notice a cottage on your left, halfway up the lane?'

'I think so. Yes, just above the sign for the stables?' Carla looked confused.

'That's where Otto and his dad live. I can't see me moving in there. If we did ever get married – and I'm not saying that we will – I think it might be more sensible for him to move in with me.'

'Live on the farm?'

'Where else?'

'Don't you miss Birmingham?'

'I did at first...' Dulcie hesitated. 'I miss my family, but not as much since Nikki and Sammy moved to Picklewick, and I've got Otto now, of course. And I miss my friends – you know you can visit anytime, don't you?'

Carla tilted her glass in Dulcie's direction in acknowledgement. 'You don't miss living in a city?'

'You mean, the noise, all those other people, the traffic?'

'The clubs, bars, shops...?'

'If I'm honest, I was getting fed up with the party lifestyle, and I couldn't really afford to go shopping much, so, no, not really. I love it here. I can't imagine living anywhere else.'

Even if she had to sell the farm tomorrow, Dulcie wouldn't dream of returning to Birmingham. She would find a little house in the village and carry on living in Picklewick.

But she had no intention of selling it. In fact, she had every intention of trying to make a go of it. She was still working the day job thankfully, which kept her head above water, but she didn't want to be a customer care advisor for the rest of her life. Ideally, she wanted the farm to pay its way, and even make a living from it so she could jack in her job. But the question was... how?

When she explained the situation to Carla, her friend was more than happy to bandy some ideas around.

'A festival site?' she suggested. 'Think Glastonbury, but smaller scale.'

'It'll have to be **much** smaller. Besides, my farm is on a hill. Anyway, don't you have to have planning permission or a licence for something like that?'

'No idea,' Carla replied, topping up their wine. 'You're probably right. The stage would roll down the hill. You could still have campers, though. I wouldn't want to **live** here, but it's a great place for a weekend – if you like that kind of thing. Personally, I'd prefer a luxury hotel and spa, but loads of people like camping. You could rent one of the fields out or put up a couple of cabins and call it glamping.'

'I like the idea of camping, but I'd have to sort out toilets and showers – and that would cost money I don't have.'

'You've got four bedrooms – how about running a B and B?'

'Maybe in the future, but not right now; no ensuite bathrooms,' she explained, pulling a face. 'We opened the orchard up to people who wanted to pick their own apples and pears the other week, and Otto tried out some of his foraged food recipes on them. It went down a storm. I just wish we could do something like that every month. I'm planning on growing pumpkins for next autumn, but that's a whole year away.'

'Lambs,' Carla said. 'Remember that city farm place we went to in year three? Or was it year four? Anyway, they had lambs.'

'A couple of people who came to the harvest festival mentioned that, but I don't like sheep. Would goats work as well, do you think?'

'I don't see why not.' Carla sat forward, excitedly. 'You could have rabbits too, and those pygmy pigs. And a donkey! I love donkeys.'

'It's the ears,' Dulcie said. 'You just want to stroke them, and the noses. Petra has one. He's called Gerald.'

'There you go! You could borrow him.'

'There's one small flaw in this petting-zoo plan,' Dulcie cautioned. 'I don't have any baby goats.'

Carla scoffed. 'You've got a **farm** – go get some!'

Easier said than done, Dulcie thought. She didn't know the first thing about breeding goats.

Suddenly she was missing Otto even more than she had been missing him already. He would know about goats, and whether Carla's idea was as daft as Dulcie suspected it might be.

As soon as he returned to Muddypuddle Lane she would ask him. After a suitably satisfying welcome home, that is!

What a day, Otto thought, as he tidied away the remains of the foodstuff he had brought with him to the shoot. He hadn't known what to expect, but it had certainly been an experience and one he wouldn't forget in a hurry.

He had arrived at the studio fully prepared to cook his dishes and for them to be photographed with some additional propping and fiddling by Fergie, the food stylist. But that was the opposite of what actually happened. Fergie had done the 'cooking', with Otto advising on what the dish should look like in real life. And as a starting point, they had explored the photographing of the infamous mushroom and mugwort soup, with Otto comparing his own efforts to those of professional shots of soups that he had found on the internet.

Fergie had shown him how it was done, and it had almost blown Otto's mind. The man had mixed agar agar with water in the bowl which was going to be used for photographing the soup, whilst Otto finely chopped a handful of mugwort leaves (he was going to have to see if the plant was known by a nicer-sounding name) and fried the mushrooms. When the agar mixture had set, the jelly-like substance almost filling the bowl completely, Fergie had piled the mushrooms on top, added a small amount of 'broth' by using a stock cube dissolved in water, to which a dash of gravy browning had been added to give it a richer look – just enough to conceal the top of the agar mixture – then he had sprinkled a pinch of chopped mugwort leaves on top for garnish. The bowl had then been artfully placed on a table, along with additional leaves, a scattering of plump mushrooms and a very shiny spoon.

Instant mashed potato and purple food colouring became Otto's bramble ice cream, with the addition of a concoction of PVA glue, and the same food colouring painted onto it so the fake ice cream looked all shiny. The only thing real about it were the blackberries, but they had been sprayed with a hair product to make them look dewy.

And that had been just the start of it! Although Otto had done his research and knew that this was what went on, it had still been a shock to see the process in action.

After a full day in the studio (it couldn't be called a kitchen as such), Otto was knackered. His wallet was also significantly lighter and he hoped it was worth it; although to be fair, the photographer had shown him image after image as she'd taken them, to ensure that he was happy with the result, although it would be several days before he received the proofs.

Finally done for the day (he had another full day tomorrow), Otto made his way back to Remi's apartment overlooking The Thames. He wanted a shower and a stiff drink, then he wanted to speak to Dulcie.

High-pitched giggles greeted him when Dulcie answered the phone and, despite his exhaustion he smiled, pleased to hear she was enjoying herself. He guessed she was tipsy, and he suspected she and her friend might have made significant inroads into the bottles of wine he had noticed in her fridge.

'I like goats,' Dulcie slurred. 'Do you like goats?'

'Um, they're okay.' He wondered what had brought this on.

'They have babies!'

'Is Princess in kid? Petra hadn't mentioned it.'

'Dunno.'

'Riiight...' That was as clear as mud, he thought, bemused.

'**We** can have babies,' Dulcie chortled.

Otto blinked. Having children wasn't something he had given much thought to, but now that Dulcie had put the idea in his head he had a sudden vision of a little girl crawling around the floor of the farmhouse. She had her mother's eyes and maybe his hair, and it brought a lump to his throat.

'Baby goats are so cute,' Dulcie was saying. 'Can we have some? **Please?**'

Ah, **that's** what she meant.

The idea of him and Dulcie having a baby lingered as he replied, 'You'll have to speak to Petra about that. Princess and Toffee belong to her.'

'I want goats of my own. Can I have some? I'll look after them, honest.'

Otto chuckled: she sounded like a kid asking for a puppy.

'And rabbits,' she added. 'People like rabbits. They've got ears and noses.'

'So they have.' He tried not to laugh. Dulcie was more than tipsy – she was three sheets to the wind. He hoped she wouldn't have too bad a hangover in the morning, and he wished he could be there to soothe her with tea and painkillers.

Missing her dreadfully, he had just put down the phone when Remi entered the apartment.

His friend threw himself into one of the leather chairs and groaned. He brought with him a faint whiff of garlic and onions. 'That was a shift from hell,' he said. 'I swear if I had the money to set up on my own, I would.'

'I thought you were taking a few days off?' Remi had still been in bed when Otto headed off to the shoot this morning.

'So did I, but I got a phone call asking me to come in.' He rolled his eyes. 'I refused to work this evening, though.'

'You could have, I wouldn't have minded.'

'And miss out on a night on the town?'

'Is that what we're doing?' Otto had to think long and hard to remember the last time he'd been 'out on the town'. At thirty-four, he had assumed that nights spent partying were behind him. Besides, he had another day of photography tomorrow, and he wasn't sure he could face it with a hangover.

He would just have to be strict and pace himself.

Oh, crap, not another shot, Otto thought, as Remi plonked a small glass of clear liquid on the table. His head was spinning already, adding to the pounding beat of the music which was so loud it reverberated in his chest. He was getting too old for this...

'Cheers!' Remi cried, downing his shot in one gulp. He slammed the empty glass on the table and turned to scan the dance floor.

Whilst Remi had his back to him, Otto hastily emptied his shot into the dregs of a pint glass on the empty table next to theirs.

It was getting late and he wanted his bed, but Remi was in full throttle and Otto remembered when he used to work hard and party hard like that, too. He might miss the work bit, but he didn't miss the partying, and he realised that living in Picklewick had changed him.

Eventually he managed to persuade Remi to leave the club and go get some food. Otto was starving, having eaten very little all day, and he dragged Remi towards a burger bar that was open all night. It wasn't far from his old stomping ground near The Fern, and he used to frequent it when he craved good, simple, tasty food after cooking elaborate meals all evening.

The burger was fat, juicy and cooked to perfection, and Otto was wolfing his down with enthusiasm, leaning against a lamppost and making noises of appreciation, when a passer-by stopped and peered at him.

Otto recognised the man at once. He had forgotten that Alistair liked walking home along this street after the restaurant closed.

'Hi, Alistair,' Otto mumbled, around a mouthful of food.

'I thought it was you.' Alistair stuck out a hand.

Otto hastily wiped his fingers on a serviette, before shaking. 'Good to see you,' he said.

Alistair pumped his arm vigorously. 'You should have told me you were back in London.'

'It's only a fleeting visit.'

Alistair's face fell. 'You're not back for good then? I was hoping you wanted your old job back.'

'Unfortunately, no.' Otto tried to sound regretful, but he didn't feel it. He had forgotten just how much of an assault on the senses being in London was. When he had first moved to the capital it had been a shock, but he had embraced it with enthusiasm and had thrown himself into everything the city had to offer. He supposed he had become immune to the hordes of people, the incessant traffic, the unrelenting noise. And don't get him started on the air quality!

'How's your father?' Alistair asked.

Otto dragged himself out of his memories. 'Getting there. He's much better now that he doesn't have the farm to worry about. How are you?' He studied his former boss. The man was in his late fifties, skinny despite being an immense foodie, snappily dressed, and thinning a little on top. He looked much the same, but with the addition of another crow's foot or two.

'I'd be better if you come back to work for me,' Alistair grumbled. 'My current head chef isn't a patch on you. I hear you're publishing a cookbook?' He raised his eyebrows.

Otto might have guessed Alistair would know – there might well be hundreds of eateries in London, but the top-notch places kept a close eye on what their rivals were up to, and gossip was rife.

'I'm giving it a go,' he said.

'Foraging?' Alistair's eyebrows remained in position.

'Yeah.'

'It's on trend,' Alistair observed. 'Let me know how it goes.' He clapped Otto on the shoulder. 'And when your father is fully recovered, let me know and you can have your old job back. Or better.' He tapped the side of his nose.

Otto had no idea what that meant. 'Good to see you, Alistair,' he said and watched him walk away, feeling unsettled.

He didn't miss working for Alistair as such, but by god he missed his kitchen. He missed the creative process of combining different ingredients and flavours together. He missed the tension of ensuring hundreds of dishes were prepared to perfection every night. He missed the sounds of people enjoying his food.

Damn it! He missed being a chef.

But he missed Dulcie more, and if he could appease his appetite for cooking wonderful food by creating new dishes for a cookery book, then that's what he would do.

But... he had already created the recipes and he now had to sell the damned thing. So what was he going to do afterwards, if he did manage to find a publisher? Could he write another cookbook, or would he have to rethink his future?

'They're not quite as sweet as I imagined they would be,' Carla said, eyeing Princess and Toffee with caution, after she had insisted on accompanying Dulcie when she let the goats out this morning. 'And I thought they'd be smaller.'

'You're thinking of baby goats,' Dulcie chuckled, then said, 'Ow,' as her head reminded her that she had drunk more wine than was good for her last night. 'I need a cup of tea, but first I'd better see to this lot.'

That was the problem with owning animals – they had to be cared for no matter how hungover the human was.

'Tea sounds good,' Carla said. 'I'm gasping. And a bacon buttie? I could eat a horse.'

'I'll just let the chickens out, then I'll make us breakfast.' Dulcie wished Otto was here to make it for them. She didn't think she could face cooking bacon right now. If she hadn't had so much to drink last night, she would have suggested going into the village for a fried breakfast, but her blood alcohol level would still be over the legal limit, and she didn't want to be arrested by Gio.

'I'm starving,' Carla reiterated, and Dulcie felt a stab of envy. She recalled being able to drink a skinful, and then wake up the following morning with just a mild headache and a raging hunger. She must be out of practice.

'I must say, I'm surprised to see you out of bed before midday,' she said to Carla. If it hadn't been for the animals, Dulcie would still be in bed feeling sorry for herself.

Carla narrowed her eyes. To Dulcie's annoyance they were clear and bright, unlike her own puffy, bloodshot peepers. 'Your bloody cockerel woke me up.'

Fred was another of Petra's animals, and he often paid a visit to Dulcie's chickens, clearly thinking they were as much his ladies as Petra's own hens were. Dulcie had become so accustomed to the racket he made that she didn't hear him anymore.

'Why is everything so loud?' Carla grumbled as she followed Dulcie into the orchard, towards the chicken coop. 'I thought it would be peaceful, but it's noisier here than in the Bullring on a Saturday night.'

Dulcie flinched as she unlatched the door to the coop, the clucking noises from inside quickly building to a crescendo as the hens realised that freedom and breakfast were imminent.

'You can hardly compare Muddypuddle Lane to Birmingham city centre,' Dulcie shouted above the noise. She hastily scattered some chicken feed in the grass, and left the excitable birds to it, breathing a sigh of relief as the frantic squawking diminished.

'I rest my case,' Carla said, glaring at the hens.

 'They're only like that because they want their breakfast. They are quiet the rest of the time.'

Carla tutted. 'That bloody cockerel wasn't quiet. And I swear someone was being murdered in the middle of the night. The noise was horrible.' She shuddered.

'I expect you heard a fox.'

'It's so bleedin' quiet here, that every noise is amplified,' Carla complained, contradicting her earlier comment. 'At least in Birmingham it all blends into one, nothing really stands out. Here you can even hear the individual cars.' She pointed in the direction of the village. 'It's not natural.'

'That's because it's coming up the lane,' Dulcie told her, catching sight of the postman's van as it trundled into the farmyard.

Ashton, the postie, got out. He was carrying a couple of letters and a small parcel, which Dulcie hoped was the make-up she liked to use but couldn't get in Picklewick. Thank god for online shopping!

'Morning.' he called cheerily, walking towards her. When he was close enough, he handed her the post. 'Here you go.'

'Thanks. Not too keen on the brown envelope, though. You can take that away with you,' Dulcie joked.

'Sorry, no can do.'

She was aware of his gaze alighting on Carla and noticed his eyes widen. Dulcie wasn't surprised: Carla often had that effect on men. Dulcie used to feel that she lived in her vivacious friend's shadow, but not any longer. Since coming to Picklewick she had grown into her skin, so to speak, which was mostly due to Otto.

He made her feel that she was the most beautiful and most special woman on earth.

With a pang, she wondered what he was doing now. Was he at the shoot yet? She had meant to ask him how it was going when she spoke to him yesterday, but she had been rather sozzled. All she could remember was wittering on about goats.

'Who was **that**?' Carla hissed as Ashton got back into his van and drove out of the farmyard.

Dulcie gave her a quizzical look. 'The postman.'

'I know that, silly. I meant, what's his name, is he married, and did you see how gorgeous he is?'

'Put your tongue away, Carla. Only yesterday you were drooling over Gio.'

'A girl can look, can't she? And you've got to admit, Gio is lush. But your postman is even lusher – if there is such a word.'

'There is now,' Dulcie said, wryly.

Carla liked to play the field. She wasn't promiscuous, in that she didn't sleep with every man she went on a date with, but she'd had more boyfriends than Dulcie could shake a stick at.

'Well? **Is** he married?'

'I've no idea.'

'You can at least tell me his name.'

'Ashton.'

'Ooh, it suits him. No wonder you like living in Picklewick if all the men look like him.'

'Remind me to introduce you to Walter and Amos.'

'Isn't Walter Otto's father?' Carla looked puzzled.

'Yes, he is.'

'That means he must be at least sixty!'

'He's in his seventies. So, no, not all men in Picklewick are lush.' To be honest, Dulcie had never looked at Ashton that way – but then, she had already met Otto, who had filled her thoughts from the very first day.

'Ashton is though,' Carla replied, dreamily.

'Down girl. Come on, let's get some breakfast inside us, then we'll take a walk into the village and mooch around the shops.' She linked arms with her best friend. 'I'll even treat you to lunch at The Black Horse.'

'What was all that talk about goats?' Otto asked. He and Dulcie were snuggled up on the sofa, watching TV in Dulcie's living room. It was Sunday evening and to his amusement Dulcie wanted to watch Countryfile. It was the first time she had shown any interest in the farming programme, and it brought to mind the drunken conversation he'd had with her earlier in the week, whilst he had been in London.

Dulcie pulled a face as she said, 'Me and Carla were trying to come up with suggestions to make the farm earn its keep, and I'm not sure which of us came up with it, but we thought a petting zoo was a good idea for the spring. You know, lambs and donkeys, a couple of rabbits... The kids had so much fun stroking Princess and Toffee during the pick-your-own fruit day that I thought I might be able to do a spring version, minus the apples and pears.' She wrinkled her cute nose. 'Then I sobered up and realised it's a daft idea.'

'Is it, though?' Otto replied thoughtfully. 'Your fields are meant to have livestock on them, and I know you don't like sheep, but you seem quite taken with Petra's goats.'

'But what happens when the baby goats grow up? I'll have to have more baby goats the following year, and the year after that, and before I know it, I'll be overrun with them.'

'You can sell them or keep them for milk. Goats' milk is big business.'

'Can't say I've ever tried it.'

'It tastes very similar to cow's milk, and it makes wonderful cheese and yoghurt. You can even make ice cream and butter with it. But – and this could be a problem – you would have to pasteurise it, and that kind of set-up costs money, not to mention the bottling process. It might be worth the initial investment, though.' He paused, then said, 'Or you could use the milk to make soap.'

Dulcie stared at him, and her eyes widened. 'Soap? **Soap!** Yes!!' She clapped her hands excitedly. 'I made soap once using a kit I had for Christmas. It was fun.' She stopped abruptly. Her mouth dropped open and she reached for her phone. Thumbs flying over the screen, she studied it. 'You can also make moisturising lotions, face wash, lip balm, candles – candles! **Yes!**' She read some more, then said, 'Do you think I should keep bees, too?'

Otto laughed; her enthusiasm was infectious and very endearing. 'One step at a time, eh? Why don't you experiment first, before you invest in your own goats? Buy some milk and the rest of the ingredients, and give soap-making a go. If you enjoy doing it and you think it will be cost effective, then you can look into owning your own animals.'

Dulcie pouted. 'Stop being so sensible.' Her nose wrinkled again, and she sighed.

'I suppose you're right. Do you want to help me make the first batch?'

'Go on, then. And if there is any milk left over, I'm sure I can use it up.'

'Ice cream?' she asked, hopefully.

'What flavour?' he began, but before she could reply, he said, 'How about hazelnut, or rosehip? I could try pumpkin flavour, seeing as Halloween isn't far away.'

'That sounds delicious.'

Otto thought it did too, but what was even more delicious was Dulcie herself. Her eyes were shining with excitement and her lips were slightly parted. He simply had to kiss her.

And it was safe to say, there was absolutely no talk of goats until some considerable time later.

CHAPTER FIVE

Dulcie eyed the assembled pile of ingredients doubtfully. She'd had to order all of it, except for the milk itself, off the internet, and every time she had seen Ashton with another parcel in his hands she'd thought of Carla.

The two of them would look good together, she acknowledged, but it was a moot point: he lived in Thornbury and Carla lived in Birmingham. But that didn't prevent Dulcie from finding out a bit more about him.

After explaining that the influx of parcels was because she was trying her hand at making soap, she had not-too-subtly suggested that he might like to give some to his wife to try, as Dulcie would need an unbiased opinion. He told her he didn't have a wife, but he did have a girlfriend, and he expected she would be delighted to give it a go.

Sorry, Carla, Dulcie had thought.

And now here she was, staring at a range of items scattered across the kitchen table and wondering if making soap was a good idea after all.

As though sensing her hesitation, Otto came up behind her and slipped his arms around her waist. The kiss on the side of her neck was comforting.

'Shall we get started?' he suggested. 'I've printed out the instructions, but don't forget, if this recipe doesn't work we can always tweak it, or try another. At this stage, it'll be trial and error.'

She was glad he was here, helping, as she was suddenly assailed by doubts; she didn't doubt that she could **make** the soap, but she doubted whether anyone would actually want to **buy** it. She hoped she hadn't wasted her money, but she supposed she could always use it herself, or give some to her sisters for Christmas.

Donning safety gear (they both wore goggles and gloves because lye was caustic and could cause a chemical burn) she and Otto worked side-by-side, measuring, stirring and mixing. She had seen Otto at work in the kitchen on numerous occasions, and he generally made a mess, but today he was being ultra tidy and careful, and she kept shooting him goggly glances, captivated by the concentration on his face.

Even though he wasn't cooking food today, it was clear that his natural home was the kitchen. He was so absorbed in his task that it made her tummy clench as she recalled her conversation with Walter. She wondered anew what Otto would do with himself once this cookbook was published. Would he immediately throw himself into the next one, or would he want to return to work in a restaurant kitchen?

She had a feeling it might be the latter: she had heard the regret in his voice when he'd recounted his chat with his former boss, and she wondered whether Otto would have taken Alistair up on his job offer if Walter **had** been back to full health.

She had a horrid feeling that he might have done, because cooking was so clearly his passion.

All she hoped was that his passion didn't take him away from Muddypuddle Lane for a second time.

But even if it didn't, she was also mindful of Otto telling her that his friend's relationship had broken up because of the unsociable hours chefs often worked. It would never happen to her and Otto, of course, but she was nevertheless aware that if he did go back into a commercial kitchen then she may very well see far less of him than she would like.

Every time his phone notified him he had an email, Otto jumped. It had been well over a week since the foodie photo shoot, and he had hoped to have had the proofs by now. He was desperate to move on with pitching to an agent, and everything else was good to go apart from the accompanying images.

Not feeling hopeful (he'd had too many false alarms over the past few days) he opened his email app, and his heart leapt when he saw it was from the photographer.

Wanting to view the images on a larger screen, he hurried home.

He had been taking Peg out for a stroll, too restless to stay indoors despite the fine drizzle and low mist, and he had been almost at the top of the hill when the notification came through. He debated detouring to see Dulcie, but she was working and he didn't want to interrupt her, so he dashed past the entrance to the farmyard and jogged down the lane, Peg gambolling at his side.

'Where's the fire?' his dad asked as he charged through the door.

'I've just been sent the photos,' Otto said, grabbing the laptop as he slid into a chair at the table.

Walter heaved himself to his feet and came to stand behind him as he opened the attachment. Otto scrolled rapidly through the photos, his heart in his mouth, and then he went back to the beginning and studied each one intently.

'Well?' his dad demanded. 'Are you pleased?'

'I love them,' Otto announced. They were brilliant; the photographer had captured the essence of each dish perfectly, and had sent him several shots of each one, taken from slightly different angles. The only problem...? He now had to choose which photo best represented each dish, and it wasn't going to be easy.

Two hours later, he had finalised his choices and his proposal was complete. The last thing to be done was a **final**, final check (as opposed to the final one he had just done), attach everything, and press send.

He had a 'favourite' agent, and he would email her first, then work his way down the list. He wasn't entirely sure of the protocol of pitching to more than one agent at a time but, damn it, he didn't think it realistic to wait for a reply from the first before he sent it to the next. He had read stories online of prospective authors waiting months and months to hear back, and he didn't have that kind of time to waste.

Otto hovered the cursor over the send button for a moment, then gathered his courage and clicked it.

There, it was done. All he could do now was keep his fingers crossed and hope the agent liked it.

Dulcie couldn't resist checking the soap again. She had taken the soap-filled mould out of the freezer this morning and it was currently sitting on the kitchen windowsill where it would live for the next three or four days. After that, she would remove the soap from the mould and then it would need to cure for four weeks – which she hadn't realised initially, having assumed it could be used straight away.

Apparently, if it wasn't left to cure, the bars wouldn't last as long, and neither would they lather up as well as they should. It was frustrating but necessary, but she didn't know if she could wait that long before she tried it.

It looked lovely and creamy though – almost good enough to eat – and it smelt divine. She had added oatmeal and honey fragranced oils, and the scent was mouth-wateringly good.

What was also mouth-wateringly good was the fudge that Otto had made with the leftover goats' milk. She had indulged in a couple of cubes for breakfast (who wouldn't?) and she had packaged up a portion to take down to Walter.

She was popping to the cottage for her tea this evening, so she took it with her. He would enjoy a couple of pieces with a cuppa after his meal, and if he was anything like her, he wouldn't be able to stop at two. The fudge was incredibly moreish.

Knocking once on the door to announce her arrival, Dulcie stepped into the warmth of the cottage and she was immediately assaulted by the smell of cooking, the heat from the open fire in the living room, and the enthusiastic welcome of a Border collie.

Laughing at the dog, who was as interested in the contents of her coat pocket as she was in being petted, Dulcie fought her way into the kitchen, taking her coat off as she did so. Otto was doing the cooking, and as usual Walter was sitting at the table, watching.

'Hi, Walter.' She gave him a kiss on his whiskery cheek, before enfolding Otto in a brief hug. 'Anything I can do?' she asked, feeling she should offer but guessing that her boyfriend would probably refuse.

Otto batted her away after giving her a kiss on the lips. He tasted of tomatoes with a hint of garlic. 'Go sit down and keep my dad company,' he told her.

Dulcie took a seat at the table.

'I've brought you some fudge,' she said, handing Walter a lavender-patterned paper bag. She had bought a supply of bags in anticipation of wrapping her soaps in them when she came to sell them. Although she knew she was being premature, the bags had been on offer and they were so pretty. She had wanted a lilac pattern, to reflect the name of the farm but she hadn't seen any. If the soap turned out okay, and there was no reason why it shouldn't, she might invest in having stickers made. She had already checked out Etsy and they were reasonable enough, and on looking through the site, she had realised that she might be able to sell her own soap there too, despite the market being crowded. Now that she had bought the moulds and the raw ingredients, there wouldn't be any further outlay. Unless... she invested in a couple of goats.

Walter sniffed at the packet of fudge. 'Smells nice. I'll have some later.' He popped it on the worktop and said, 'Otto has sent his query off to an agent.'

'I know, he messaged me to say he'd sent it.' He'd also forwarded the photos to her so she could take a look. They were very good, but she still couldn't believe that most of the food was actually fake or covered in something inedible.

'I don't expect to hear anything for weeks,' Otto said, gloomily.

'What will you do if you don't hear back soon, or if they pass?' she wanted to know.

'Keep sending it off to agents.' He shrugged. 'In the meantime, I suppose I'd better start looking for paid employment.'

Walter gave his son a keen glance. 'Cheffing?'

'It's what I do. I don't know anything else.'

Dulcie knew that even if he did, Otto wouldn't want to do anything other than cook. 'Have you started looking?'

'A bit. There's nothing in Picklewick obviously, but I've had a quick trawl through the vacancies in Thornbury.' He didn't look happy, and she suspected he hadn't seen anything suitable.

It would be hard for a chef of his calibre to find work. He had tried earlier in the year, asking Dave, the landlord of The Black Horse in the village, if there were any jobs going in the kitchen. Dulcie had inadvertently overheard Dave say that even if he did have a position that needed filling, he would be wary of employing a Michelin star chef to fill it.

Walter, bless him, tried to lighten his son's mood. 'I keep saying, he ought to open his own place here in Picklewick. He could please himself then and cook what he likes.'

'I'm not sure I'd want to do that, Dad. Not only is it a hell of a commitment, it's also a hell of an outlay. I haven't got the money.' He said it gently, but Walter still flinched.

'I'm sorry, Otto. If it hadn't been for my stupidity, you'd have a farm to sell.'

Otto stopped what he was doing, walked over to his dad and put an arm around his shoulders. 'Stop beating yourself up over it. What's done is done. Anyway,' he shot Dulcie a glance. It was so full of love that her heart turned to mush. 'If we hadn't raffled off the farm, I never would have met Dulcie, so you should give yourself a pat on the back for that.'

'True…' Walter said, slowly. Although Dulcie could tell that the elderly gent wasn't totally convinced, at least he didn't look as unhappy as he had a few seconds ago.

Otto went back to the hob and the pans which were bubbling away on them. Her tummy rumbled, and she couldn't wait to see what he had made. He wasn't focusing on foraged ingredients anymore, and now had the whole of the local supermarket to choose from.

Typically, he had refused to tell her, aware that she often had preconceived ideas of what she liked and what she didn't. It had only taken a couple of instances where she had turned her nose up at something because she didn't like the sound of it, only to be surprised to discover that she actually liked it, for him to not tell her what was in a dish until she had tasted it and had given her verdict.

'I hear you're thinking of keeping goats,' Walter said. 'I knew you wouldn't be able to resist having some livestock.' He looked so pleased with himself that Dulcie grinned.

'No sheep,' she warned. 'Just goats, and that's not for definite. It all depends on how well the soap making goes.'

'We'll make a farmer out of you yet,' the old man declared. 'How many chickens have you got now?'

'Nine. Do you need any more eggs?'

'We've still got some left from last week.'

'I can't use nine eggs a day, although one or two have stopped laying. Is that normal?'

'It is,' Walter informed her. 'The drop in temperature and the decreasing daylight tells them to stop laying. If you want them to carry on, you need to bring them inside and give them more heat and light.'

'Inside – as in, **in the house**?' Over Dulcie's dead body! She liked her chickens, but not enough to have them strutting around her sitting room.

Walter nearly fell off his chair with laughter. 'In the **barn** with a light bulb and plenty of feed. But you might want to give them a rest – laying eggs takes a lot out of a bird. If you do decide to rest them, don't worry about not having any eggs – just stockpile them for a few weeks beforehand. Eggs will stay fresh for up to two months in a sealed container in the fridge (just don't wash them) or you can freeze them. Not the whole egg,' he added hastily when Dulcie opened her mouth. 'You have to separate the yolks from the whites. Use ice cube trays. They work a treat.'

It seemed like an awful lot of effort, but maybe she would give it a go. However, she might just bring the hens into the barn anyway before it got much colder – more for her sake than for theirs, because she was already shivering at the thought of traipsing out to the orchard on dark and cold December mornings.

Suddenly a lightbulb went off in her head. She could have baby chicks to go with the baby goats and the rabbits she had yet to look into keeping. She'd had a guinea pig when she was younger, so maybe rabbits weren't too dissimilar.

Dulcie hadn't quite formed a picture of what her farm would look like next year, but she had begun making an outline. So far, she'd only pencilled in a couple of things, such as a spring petting corner (she could hardly keep referring to it as a zoo) and the autumn fruit picking combined with a harvest festival and pumpkin patch, but she was getting there.

Realising it would involve a tremendous amount of hard work, Dulcie knew she had some tough months ahead – but with Walter's knowledge and experience (he **was** the farmer after all) and Otto's support and level head (he would be able to talk some sense into her if she came up with a truly ridiculous idea), she might, **just might**, be able to make this little farm of hers work.

CHAPTER SIX

This feels more like a fun day out than a business trip, Dulcie thought, as she gazed out of the window of Petra's Land Rover. She was sitting in the back, squashed between Otto and Walter, and Amos was in the passenger seat. The vehicle smelled vaguely of horse and manure – or was the niff coming from Petra, who had just confessed to mucking out a stable or two and was still wearing grubby jodhpurs and dirty boots.

Dulcie kept glancing at the space behind the rear seats and wondering if it was large enough for a goat. She was fairly certain it wouldn't be big enough for more than one, and as she was planning on purchasing at least three or four animals, she was already worrying about how she was going to transport them from the breeder they were currently on their way to see.

The suspension in the Land Rover wasn't the best, and her teeth rattled as the vehicle bounced along a track. But as they drew nearer to their destination her excitement grew when she caught her first glimpse of goats in a field.

'Look, they've got a playground!' she cried in astonishment, seeing a couple of the creatures climbing up planks of wood balanced on what looked like enormous cotton reels, which she assumed must have once held lengths of pipe or copper wire. A three-tiered lookout post had been constructed out of pallets, and there was even some kind of large swinging platform and a seesaw.

'They get bored easily, do goats,' Amos warned. 'If you don't give them something to occupy them, they'll get up to all kinds of mischief.'

'Ooh, I want a goaty playground,' she said, turning to Otto. 'Can you help me make one?'

Otto rolled his eyes and sighed. 'If I must.' He softened his words with a kiss.

'Give it a rest,' Petra muttered. 'I wouldn't have offered to bring you if I knew you were going to get all lovey-dovey.'

'Have you and Harry had a row?' Amos asked. He scooted around to speak to Dulcie. 'Those two squabble like a cat and dog. He wants to offer riding holidays by turning the old sheep shed into a kind of hostel, but Petra's having none of it.'

'I've got enough on my plate as it is,' Petra grumbled. 'And the way Harry is carrying on, we won't have a barn left for the actual horses.'

'The horses live in the stable block,' Amos pointed out.

'Yes, but I still need a barn...'

Thankfully the discussion came to an end as Petra parked the Land Rover, and everyone got out.

A man walked towards them. He was leading a goat, who had a leather collar around its neck, and Dulcie suppressed a squeal. It was very small, and at first she thought it was a baby, until Otto said in her ear, 'That's a full-grown pygmy goat, in case you're wondering.'

'The babies must be **tiny**,' Dulcie hissed back.

'They are, and they're incredibly cute.'

'I want one. Can pygmy goats be milked?'

'Dunno, but here's the man to ask.'

Petra shook hands with the guy, who introduced himself as Mike. 'I bought Princess from you,' she reminded him, 'And last year, you had her back to put to one of your billies. Got a nice little kid from her.'

'Are you thinking of breeding from her again?' he asked.

'I did consider it, but two goats are more than enough, and if Dulcie does go ahead

with her plan, I can buy all the milk I
need from her.'

'Okay, shall we take a look at some of the
females I've got available?' He turned to
Dulcie. 'Petra says you're wanting a
couple of goats for milk. Have you got
any particular breed in mind?'

Dulcie had done a bit of research, but she
had found it rather contradictory, with
some people championing one breed, and
others effusing the pros of another. So,
she had an open mind and was hoping
that Mike would give her the benefit of
his wisdom once she'd told him what she
wanted.

This, he was more than happy to do, and
after wandering around the pens and
stroking goat after goat, Dulcie settled on
three white ones of a breed renowned for
their milk yield and calm temperament,

and two light brown ones which were also good milkers but were more famous for the quality of the cheese.

And of course, she couldn't resist a couple of pygmy goats. Three in fact... So she ended up buying eight goats in total – more than she had anticipated, but those little ones were simply gorgeous. She had also spent far more than she had intended, but everyone would adore those pygmies, and even if there weren't any goatlings on the farm just yet (she much preferred the word 'goatling' to 'kid', when referring to baby goats, despite suspecting she might have made it up herself), these loveable little creatures looked like babies because of their small stature.

'Do you deliver?' she asked, once again wondering how she was going to transport them from here to Muddypuddle Lane.

Mike said, 'I do. But we've got plenty of time to organise that.'

'We have? Can't you deliver next week?'

'Not if you want to ensure they are in kid. These were bred only a few weeks ago, so it'll be another month or two yet before we'll know for sure whether they are pregnant or not.'

'Oh.' Dulcie was crestfallen. 'What if they're not?'

'Because you are purchasing them on the understanding that they are in kid, if one of them proves not to be pregnant, you can choose another that most definitely is.'

'I see.' She brightened. 'I suppose it will give me time to build a playground for them.'

'They'll need a shelter, too,' Walter advised. He gave Amos a look. 'Fancy giving me a hand with that?'

'Dad!' Otto glared at his father. 'You are in no fit state to do any building work.'

'It's just nailing a few planks of wood together,' Walter protested. 'I'm sure me and Amos can manage that between us.'

Otto shook his head. 'I can't believe I'm hearing this. You're supposed to be taking it easy.'

'I've taken it easy for months. If you think I'm going to vegetate in that chair until I draw my last breath, you can think again.'

'He's feeling better,' Otto said to no one in particular.

'I've been feeling better for a while, son,' Walter shot back. 'It'll do me good to have something I can get my teeth into. I'll feel useful again.' He stopped and stared at Dulcie, 'That is, if you don't mind a bit of help. I don't want to tread on your toes.'

Dulcie, feeling very much as though she was caught between a rock and a hard place, sent Otto a helpless look. She didn't want to encourage Walter if Otto didn't approve. It had taken Walter a long time to regain his health and his strength, and she didn't want to be responsible for any relapse. On the other hand, she could tell that Walter was chomping at the bit and was getting very fed up with not having much to do. It must be hard for him to go from running the farm singlehandedly, to being an invalid and dependent on Otto, so she took it as a good sign that the old man wanted to involve himself in the farm he used to own.

Otto caught her eye. He sighed and shrugged. 'It's up to you,' he said to his dad. 'Just don't overdo it. I'll help too – it'll give me something to do.'

Something to do whilst he was waiting for a response from one of the agents, Dulcie thought. And something to do whilst he was looking for a job. Because with Walter clearly so much better, Otto was now free to find a role as a head chef, doing what he loved most in the world.

'The evenings are drawing in,' Otto observed a couple of days later. It was the first of November and the leaves had already tuned colour, the dramatic displays of ochre, crimson and orange clearly visible in the valley below.

Crisp, clear autumn days were great for taking long walks in the hills above the farm, and he and Dulcie had filled a flask with hot chocolate, and he had thrown together a picnic of pasties that he had baked earlier whilst waiting for Dulcie to finish work for the day, along with some individual pumpkin pies. Before much longer, it would be too dark to go walking in the hills in the evenings, so he had been determined to make the most of it. Waiting didn't suit him, and Otto found he was restless more often than not, so he had been finding things to do to keep busy.

Work had begun on the shelter in the goats' field, with Otto keeping a stern eye on Walter to make sure he wasn't exerting himself too much. But with Otto insisting that his dad and Amos take their time, they were only doing a couple of hours a day, leaving Otto trying to find something to do to fill the rest of it. Hence the baking earlier today, and the walk he and Dulcie were on now.

Anyway, it was good for both of them to get out in the fresh air. Poor Dulcie was stuck behind a desk for seven hours a day (her dining room table actually, but the principle was the same) so it was nice for her to stretch her legs.

Dulcie gazed across the valley, her hands on her hips as she caught her breath. 'That hill is always steeper than I think it's going to be,' she puffed.

'I know what you mean. I used to be able to sprint to the top of it when I was a kid. And come back down on a tea tray or a piece of cardboard. It was great fun.' He smiled wistfully then gave her a speculative look, wondering whether she would be up for doing something like that. Not today obviously, because he wasn't in the habit of carrying tea trays or large pieces of cardboard around with him. But perhaps they could come up here another time and—

She must have guessed what he was thinking, because she said, 'Oh, no, you don't! You're not talking me into sliding back down on a bit of plastic. I'll walk, thank you.'

'You're no fun,' he grumbled. He was teasing; Dulcie was a great deal of fun, especially when she was in his arms.

Dulcie must have read his mind again, because she turned to face him, snaking her hands around his waist and working them underneath his jacket until she touched the bare skin of his back. He flinched at the chill of her fingers.

'So you don't think I'm any fun, do you?' she murmured, her lips on his neck, her hands caressing their way down the small of his back towards the waistband of his jeans.

Otto closed his eyes in pleasure at her touch, wondering just how far she was going to take things. He was up for a spot of outdoor loving if she was, despite the chill in the air and their elevated position on the hillside...

Damn and blast – his phone was ringing.

Reluctantly, Otto pulled away from Dulcie with an apologetic twist of his lips, and took his phone out.

It wasn't a number he recognised and he guessed it was one of those nuisance calls everyone seemed to get at some point. If it was, he would give them a piece of his mind. But on the other hand, it could be the hospital or—

'Hello?' His voice was hesitant.

'Hi, my name is Yvette Holmes, and I'm calling from Holmes Literary Agency. Am I speaking to Otto York?'

Otto swallowed, his mouth suddenly dry. His heart was in his throat and he coughed to clear the lump that had formed there. 'Yes, this is he.' God, he sounded officious. 'I mean, yes, I'm Otto. Hi.' Now he sounded like a muppet.

'I've got your proposal in front of me, and I wondered if we could have a chat?'

'Yes, of course. What about?' Oh, for goodness sake! He was making a right idiot of himself, but she had caught him off guard, when his mind had been focused on something else entirely. 'I mean, I know what it's about, I think...' Or did he? Did agents phone to say thanks but no thanks? He closed his eyes and wished he had let the call go to answerphone, so he would have had time to prepare.

The woman chuckled. 'The possibility of my company representing you? Yes. Are you free any time this week?'

Representing me? His heart was hammering so hard, she surely must be able to hear it. He was aware of Dulcie slipping her hand into his, and he gave it a squeeze. 'Er, yes. I can be.' **Can be**? He had absolutely nothing else lined up whatsoever.

'How about Friday? Say ten-thirty? Is that good for you?'

It was perfect. Any day or time would be perfect.

The agent said, 'Fantastic! I'll email you to confirm. I'm looking forward to meeting you.'

'Me, too. Thank you.'

'By the way,' Yvette said before she ended the call. 'The images you sent were very nice. Very professional. See you Friday,' and with that she hung up.

Otto stared at the screen for a second, to make sure she really had gone, then he looked at Dulcie. 'That was Yvette

Holmes, from Holmes Literary Agency. She wants to meet me on Friday.' He slapped a hand to his forehead. 'We're supposed to be going to see the Bonfire Night fireworks in the village, aren't we? Oh, heck. Sorry, I forgot.'

'This is far more important than watching the fireworks,' Dulcie said. 'I'm so proud of you.' She was beaming from ear to ear. 'What time is your meeting?'

'Ten-thirty.'

'Then stop fretting. You should be back in plenty of time. But even if you aren't, it doesn't matter.'

'Promise me you'll go anyway? I know you've been looking forward to it.' On Halloween Dulcie had been like a big kid, decorating the house with fake cobwebs and bunting, and she had insisted on buying pumpkins to carve, which she had then taken to the stables to decorate the arena because Petra had arranged a party for her younger riders – involving horses, of course.

'If you're not back by the time it starts, I'll go with Nikki and Gio,' Dulcie said. 'They're taking Sammy, so I'm sure they won't mind if I tag along. You can either meet me there or I'll see you back at the farm.' She grabbed hold of his hand and began to tug him down the hill.

Otto asked, 'Where are we going? We haven't eaten our picnic yet.'

'The pasties will keep until tomorrow. We're going out to celebrate.'

He hung back. 'I think you might be a bit premature.'

'Don't be daft! That woman isn't going to drag you all the way to London and waste her valuable time just to tell you she's not interested. Otto, my gorgeous, wonderful man – you've got yourself an agent!'

CHAPTER SEVEN

Otto hadn't been expecting to return to London quite so soon. He had assumed it would be months before he visited the city again, but here he was – on the train this time, because driving into the centre was a nightmare and he'd had enough of that the other week.

He was feeling nervous and hadn't been able to face breakfast. The early start hadn't helped, either. He'd been up well before dawn to drive to Thornbury to catch the train. Wishing he'd had enough wits about him to suggest a slightly later time to meet, he took a deep breath and told himself to stay calm.

It was easier said than done, because he'd been on edge all week. He knew it was logical to assume that Yvette Holmes was going to offer to represent him, but until he had the contract in his hand he couldn't allow himself to believe it was actually happening. He kept thinking of all the things that could go wrong – maybe the agent wouldn't like him when she met him; maybe they'd want to change significant parts of the book. Maybe... actually, he couldn't think of anything else that could go wrong, but that didn't mean to say it wouldn't.

Cross with himself, he shook his head. This nervousness and uncertainty wasn't like him at all. He was usually confident and self-assured, but he was so far out of his comfort zone that he may as well be on another planet. If he was being asked for a demonstration of his cooking, that would be a different matter entirely.

When his phone rang, his first thought was it was Yvette calling to cancel, but when he saw it was Alistair, his curiosity was piqued.

'My goodness, Alistair, I don't speak to you for months then I get to hear your dulcet voice twice in a matter of weeks,' Otto said. 'Is there anything wrong?'

'Nothing, everything is tip-top.'

'Glad to hear it,' Otto replied.

'I wondered if we could have a chat?'

Otto had a feeling of déjà vu. Alistair was the second person this week who wanted to have a 'chat' with him. 'If it's to offer me my old job back, you already did that, and I turned you down,' he said with a chuckle. He was about to say something else, but at that moment the train went through a tunnel.

When the call reconnected, he could hear Alistair grumbling, 'Otto? Otto? Damn it, he's hung up on me.'

Otto smiled and said, 'I'd never hang up on you. The train went through a tunnel. I'm on my way to London.'

'You've not been poached by Trent Manning, have you?'

'No, definitely not.' Trent and Alistair were bitter culinary rivals. Neither of them was a chef in their own right, but both of them owned a restaurant.

'Who, then?'

'No one. Not that it's any of your business, you nosey old fart, but I've got a meeting with an agent.'

'That cookbook of yours is growing wings, is it? Well done. And while I admit to being a fart, less of the old, please.'

'Did you ring for anything in particular, or just to listen to me giving you abuse?'

'I want a chat with you.'

'So you said. What about?'

'How long will you be in London?'

'Just for the day.'

'Phone me when you're out of your meeting. I'll clear my diary for the afternoon.'

'Can't you tell me what it's about now?'

'I'd rather tell you face-to-face.'

Otto agreed to call him once he was done, on the condition that Alistair took him for lunch. They arranged to eat at The Fern, although Otto knew he would feel strange going back there as a customer and not as Head Chef.

He and Alistair had a funny relationship, Otto mused as he settled back for the rest of the journey. Alistair never minded that Otto was outspoken, and he treated Otto more as an equal than an employee. When it came to food, Otto had always expected Alistair to follow his advice – why else employ a top-notch chef if you weren't prepared to bow to their skill and experience?

But when it came to the business side of running the restaurant, Otto hadn't had any say in the matter and neither had he wanted to. The arrangement had suited them both and had been a successful one – until Otto had ended it, through no fault of his or Alistair's. If Walter hadn't needed him, Otto was fairly sure he would still be Head Chef at The Fern now.

But that chapter of his life was over, and he had a whole new book to concentrate on – **literally!** And he spent the rest of the journey between worrying about his forthcoming meeting with Yvette, and trying to figure out why Alistair was being so mysterious.

Dulcie was unable to settle, despite taking call after call from customers needing help. Or wanting to vent or complain. She did her best, but not all issues could be resolved, and some people just wanted to have a good old shout at anyone in the company.

After dealing with a particularly nasty customer who had hung up on her after calling her a rude word, she desperately needed to hear a friendly voice. She had sent Otto several messages whilst he was travelling, but it was so close to the time of his meeting that she didn't dare phone. Besides, he needed to concentrate on that, not be distracted by her moaning.

Nikki was the other obvious choice, and as it was half term and she wouldn't be in school, her poor sister was it.

'I'm keeping my fingers crossed for him,' Nikki said, after Dulcie had offloaded her angst and the conversation had swung around to Otto's imminent meeting.

Dulcie checked the time – he should be there now. She wondered how long it would be before she heard from him.

'Message me as soon as you've got any news,' Nikki said. 'I've got to go, I'm in the middle of doing the weekly shop. Will we see you later at the firework display?'

'I was meaning to ask – Otto should be back in time, but if he isn't, can I come with you?'

'Hopefully you'll be at home celebrating,' Nikki whispered, her tone wicked.

'I hope we **will** have something to celebrate, but I really want to go to the display. You know how much I love fireworks.'

'I would have thought you and Otto would produce plenty of sparks of your own!'

'Ha, ha! I'd better let you get on with your grocery shop, and I'd better get some work done. Before you go, have you thought about what you're going to do for Christmas? Will you be staying in Picklewick, or will you go spend it at Mum's?'

'I want to see Mum, Maisie and Jay, but Picklewick is our home now and I'm not sure whether Gio would be able to come with us. He'll probably have to work at least one shift over the festive season, and probably a lot more.'

Dulcie wasn't keen on leaving Picklewick either, because she guessed Otto would be torn between wanting to spend Christmas with her, and not wanting to leave Walter on his own. At least Mum had Maisie and Jay: if Otto went to

Birmingham with her, poor Walter would have no one.

'I've got an idea!' she cried. 'I'm going to ask Mum, Maisie and Jay if they'd like to spend Christmas at the farm.'

'Fantastic! A huge family Christmas – that'll be lush! I assume Jay will be home for Christmas?'

'I don't see why not – he hasn't missed one yet. Any idea which country he's in?' Dulcie asked.

'He's still in Asia, but I'm not sure exactly where,' Nikki replied. 'Whoever knew there would be such a demand for acoustic sensors!'

Jay was passionate about the environment and worked for a company who installed listening equipment in the jungle that monitored the health of the ecosystem and listened for illegal logging activity. Dulcie was immensely proud of her brother, but wished she could see more of him. He always came home for Christmas though, and she was looking forward to his visit.

Dulcie returned to work in a lighter frame of mind. She kept telling herself that she didn't have to do this job for the rest of her working life, and that it was simply a means to bring in some income until the farm paid its own way. As long as she could blow off steam now and again, she'd be fine.

Apart from the job, her life was looking particularly rosy. She had taken the first steps to making the farm profitable (she couldn't wait to welcome the goats to their new home, but that would be several weeks away yet), she was madly in love with the most gorgeous man in the world, and she had fireworks and Christmas to look forward to.

All that was needed to put the icing on top of the cake, was for Otto to get himself an agent. And she had total faith that was happening right now!

Yvette Holmes looked exactly like her photo on the company's website, although she was shorter than Otto was expecting, the top of her head only reaching to his shoulder. Her small stature aside, she had plenty of gravitas to make her presence felt, and as she walked across the foyer to greet him, he noticed several pairs of eyes following her progress.

Holmes Literary Agency had offices on the third floor of a modern building, and he hadn't expected her to come greet him herself when he had given his name to the chap on the reception desk. It was a nice touch, and he hoped it was a sign that the meeting was going to be all he prayed it would be.

'So it's you I've got to blame for the food at The Fern not being as good as it used to be,' was her opening gambit.

'Er...' Otto shook the hand she offered, wondering what he was supposed to say to that. He had included his credentials as part of the pitching process, so agents would realise he was a bona fide chef, but it hadn't occurred to him that Yvette Holmes might have dined at The Fern.

'Just teasing,' she said. 'Although I'm telling the truth when I say I was a little disappointed. The food was good, but not **as** good.'

'Thanks. I think.'

'Take it as the compliment it's meant to be.' She walked him over to the lift and pressed the button. The doors pinged open immediately, and when he gestured for her to go ahead of him, he took a moment to study her.

Wearing a black trouser suit and a cream blouse, with slicked back grey hair and pink lipstick, she looked every inch a successful businesswoman.

The company's offices were open-plan, bright, and busy, and he received a few curious glances as he followed her into a spacious office at the far end, and nervously took the seat she indicated at the conference table. A folder was waiting for her, and without preamble, she opened it. Otto caught a glimpse of a photo which he recognised as being one of his. She must have printed it out.

'I'm interested in representing you,' she began. 'But before we discuss contracts, I want to hear from you what your hopes for your book are – besides being an international bestseller.'

That **was** what he had been hoping for, even if he would never say so out loud. Wasn't that every author's dream? However, he was realistic enough to understand that a book about foraging in the British countryside wouldn't find much of a market in Australia, for instance.

'I'd like to see it on the shelves in Waterstones,' he said, after a pause. 'I'd like it to be **the** go-to recipe book for gardeners and foragers. We need to start thinking about eating what grows in our gardens, and not be so reliant on imported or mass-farmed foods.'

'I like your passion for your subject,' Yvette said, steepling her hands under her chin as she studied him.

Otto felt like a pupil sitting in front of a headteacher, and was rather unnerved. 'My passion is for cooking,' he said. 'Foraging is second to that. No matter what the ingredients are, or where they come from, taste is paramount.'

'I quite agree. Now, if this was a book on foraging, with the recipes as more of an afterthought, I would suggest going with what you just said. But as this is a cookbook, we need to focus on the recipes first and foremost. I'm only saying this, because we need to be on the same page. I have to have a clear vision of what the book is about if I'm to sell it to a publisher.' She smiled at him. 'I think it might fly, but—'

Here we go, Otto thought. There was bound to be a 'but', and he prepared himself for the worst – she liked it, but not enough to... blah, blah, blah.

She said, 'It's going to take a great deal of work on your part. Publishing a book isn't as simple as stocking it on shelves. To give it any chance of success you're going to have to actively promote it. You will be expected to do a significant amount of marketing in the form of appearances, cooking demonstrations at food festivals, persuading your peers to review it, and so on. Not only that, but the whole process, beginning with me becoming your agent to the book being bought by a reader, could take up to two years. And please don't expect much of an advance: you're not well known enough in publishing circles for that, plus it will take a while to earn out any advance before you receive a penny in royalties. Now, the reason I'm telling you this is that if I agree to take you on, I need to know you understand the process and what a publisher will expect of you.' She shuffled the contents of the folder around and brought out a document he didn't recognise. 'Are you ready to talk contracts, or do you want to think about what I've said?'

'Talk,' he said, without hesitation. He had invested a great deal of time and effort into getting this far, and to be offered a contract by his first-choice agent was a dream come true, even if she had tried her best to rain on his parade. However, he appreciated her honesty and her transparency, and realised she was doing her best to manage his expectations.

But after he had read the contract and signed on the dotted line, the euphoria he had hoped to feel was dulled by the knowledge that he couldn't afford to wait years for the book to be published. He needed an income **now**.

So it was with bitter-sweet feelings that he messaged Dulcie to tell her the 'good' news; he'd leave the not-so-good news until he spoke to her in person. Although he was proud of himself for getting this far, he was disillusioned and disheartened by the knowledge that he would have to look for a job after all. And sooner, rather than later.

He would get today out of the way, then spend the weekend scouring the various catering job sites. Something was bound to come up. It had to.

Dulcie read the message, her heart swelling with pride. Otto had done it! He had been signed by an agent. Woo hoo!

She tore her headphones off, leapt from her chair and danced around the dining room, squealing at the top of her voice. This was the best news ever! They would **really** have something to celebrate tonight.

When she had calmed down, she replied to his message, telling him how much she loved him and how proud she was of him. She would have preferred to speak to him, but she didn't like to phone in case he was still at the agency, ironing out the details or whatever it was that was being discussed. She would wait for him to phone her.

What time train do you think you'll catch? she wrote. She couldn't wait to see him.

He replied immediately. **Got a few things to wrap up. Not sure yet. I'll let you know later.**

Dulcie supposed she would have to be satisfied with that.

Unable to keep still and wanting to share the brilliant news, she phoned Nikki, who was equally as thrilled, then she called her mum.

Her mother was as pleased as punch, and even Maisie, who was at home (**no job to go to, Maisie?**), was delighted. Finally, she sent Carla a quick message, and received one back that contained nothing more than a list of emojis and a big kiss at the end. She wondered whether she should pop down the hill and tell Walter, but she guessed Otto would have already shared the good news with him.

What happens now? Dulcie wondered. Otto had been rather vague about the next stage of the publishing process, possibly because he hadn't been totally sure himself, but she was excited to find out.

It was all coming together for them, she thought. Her with the farm, Otto with the cookbook. And Walter was making steady progress health-wise. So maybe it was time to ask Otto if he would like to move in with her...?

They may have only known each other for a smidge over six months, but she knew he was the man she wanted to spend the rest of her life with. Why delay? He spent more time at the farmhouse than he did at the cottage, so living together was the next step.

She would ask him tonight, after they'd had a private celebration. Ideally, she would like **him** to ask **her**, but theirs was a weird situation. He could hardly ask her to move into the cottage with him and his dad, and she knew he would never suggest her selling the farm and getting a place together. And neither would he ask to move in with her. Therefore, it was up to her to make the first move, and tonight was the night to do it. It would be the start of their new life together, as a proper couple – and she simply couldn't wait!

Otto felt bad for not speaking to Dulcie in person and explaining the realities of the situation, but he just couldn't face her. He'd have a good chat with her this evening and explain that although the news was positive in that he had an agent, there would be a long way to go yet before he would realise any income from the book – if he ever did, because there was no guarantee a publisher would want it. He would also tell her about his plans to get a job.

As far as disasters went, it wasn't a major one, but he hoped his and Dulcie's relationship wouldn't go the same way as Remi and Steff's. Still, he supposed being a chef was no worse than any other job involving shifts and other people managed just fine, so maybe he was being overly dramatic. It wasn't as though she lived miles away and he would only get to see her now and again. She lived a short walk up the lane...

Despite the pep talk, Otto was feeling rather more sorry for himself than he should considering the circumstances, as he walked into The Fern half an hour later. It was already twelve-thirty and he hoped lunch wouldn't take long as he had a three-hour train journey ahead of him. It was doubtful whether he'd get back to Picklewick before six o'clock as it was, and he was desperate to give Dulcie a hug.

There were many familiar faces amongst the serving staff, he was relieved to discover, as he stepped inside the restaurant, and as everyone flocked around to say hello a pang went through him. It felt like coming home to be back in The Fern again – little had changed, and he soaked up the atmosphere of the front of house area where he had spent many a night after the restaurant had closed, discussing the menu with Alistair.

The man himself appeared from the direction of the kitchen, his arms open in welcome, and he drew Otto into him and gave him a patted-back hug.

'How did your meeting go?' his old boss asked as he showed Otto to the best table in the house.

'I've got an agent,' Otto said, putting on a big smile.

'Congratulations! This calls for champagne!' Alistair clapped his hands.

'No, really, I don't—'

'Bernard, open a bottle of Louis Roederer Cristal,' he instructed the maitre'd.

Like the professional that he was, Bernard didn't even flinch at the exorbitant gesture: he simply nodded, leaving Otto bemused.

'It's not that big a deal,' he said when Bernard was out of earshot, and he went on to tell Alistair about the realities of the situation.

'Nonsense! You are one step closer to publication. I have heard that getting an agent is the hardest part.' Alistair leant to the side a fraction to allow Bernard to pour the champagne, which he did with a dramatic flourish.

Otto sniffed it appreciatively, took a small mouthful and let the sparkling liquid sit on his tongue for a moment as he revelled in the flavour and the way the bubbles discretely popped in his mouth. It was delicious, and so it should be at that price.

'This is overkill,' he said, raising his glass. 'House white would have done.'

Alistair smiled. 'I have something to celebrate too.' He gently put his glass on the table, glanced around, then leant forward and said, 'I am the proud owner of two additional restaurants.' He looked incredibly pleased with himself. 'You are the first to know, and I would appreciate it if you kept it under your hat for a while.'

'Of course. Congratulations.' Otto took another sip of the wine. It was incredibly good, and he had to stop himself from gulping it down. As well as being crass, such a wine demanded to be savoured. 'Where?'

Alistair said, 'In London, obviously, but the locations are secret for the moment.'

Otto smiled. 'Why so hush-hush?'

'They are going to be sister-restaurants to The Fern, and I want only the best so I'll be poaching all the best staff.'

Uh-oh...

'That's what I wanted to talk to you about,' Alistair continued.

Otto was shaking his head. 'I've told you, I'm not coming back to London to live.'

'Not even to be my Menu Director?'

'**What?**'

'Each restaurant will have its own distinctive menu, using only the very best ingredients, prepared by the very best chefs. I need someone who I can trust to create the menus, and to make sure they are delivered to the very highest standard.' Alistair leaned forward again, his expression serious. 'Come work for me, Otto. You will have total autonomy in the kitchens, from which pans to use, to who will be the head chef in each one. You will have full control. I trust you to put each restaurant on the map. By this time next year, I fully expect all of them to have a star. After that, they will have another...' He stopped talking, but his eyes remained on Otto's face.

'I don't know what to say,' Otto murmured, after a long pause.

'Say yes. I'll even throw in an apartment to sweeten the deal, unless you still have yours?'

'I sold it.' Before Otto was aware of the full extent of the farm's debts, he had hoped that the equity from his apartment would have covered them, so he had put it on the market and had received an offer almost immediately. When it had become apparent that the money raised from the sale of his property would be nowhere near enough, it had been too late to pull out of the sale. Instead, he had used the proceeds to renovate the cottage on Muddypuddle Lane, with enough left over to keep him solvent for a while.

'There'll be a good salary, too,' Alistair said, and when he named a figure, Otto thought he must have misheard.

'Bloody hell, Alistair, that's almost three times what I earned as your head chef.'

'I know. But I've learnt that if you want the best you have to pay for it.'

'You could get Rachel Humphrey or Hugo Maitland for that.' Then Otto backtracked. 'Okay, maybe not either of those two, but you could get some serious skill for what you're offering.'

Alistair was shaking his head. 'I want **you**. I know how you operate, and I trust you. That counts for a lot.'

'My name isn't big enough, it's not enough of a draw.'

'It will be – and with this book of yours coming out...'

'It's a recipe of foraged ingredients,' Otto argued. 'There won't be any tie-in with your restaurants.'

But then Alistair said something that turned Otto's objection on its head.

'One of them will serve only foraged and locally sourced food. Would that help your book sales, hmm?'

CHAPTER EIGHT

Disappointment flooded through Dulcie as she read Otto's last message, telling her that he wouldn't be back in Picklewick until later this evening and that she should go to the firework display without him.

She wondered what was keeping him there, but when she tried to call him he didn't answer.

Feeling as though she was being clingy and needy, she tried not to phone Walter, but she couldn't help herself.

'Have you heard from Otto?' she asked.

'Not since this morning. He said he might be late back as he had bumped into Alistair – the chap who owns The Fern – and is having lunch with him.'

Dulcie knew who Alistair was, and a frisson of unease travelled through her. Why hadn't Otto phoned and told her? She would have understood. If he could find the time to call his dad, surely he could have found the time to give her a quick bell?

Telling herself not to be silly, she thought about it rationally. Walter didn't own a mobile phone and neither did he use the internet much. She didn't know whether he actually had an email address, so, apart from sending a letter, Otto had no other way of getting in contact with his dad: he **had** to phone him. Whereas he and Dulcie had already messaged each other several times today, so maybe he didn't think it was necessary to speak to her in person. He was a bloke, and in Dulcie's admittedly limited experience, blokes didn't feel the need to talk as often.

Feeling better about it (why shouldn't he meet up with Alistair? after all, he had seen Remi the last time he was in London...) Dulcie sent Nikki a quick text to tell her sister that she would meet her at the entrance to the park where the firework display was being held, then she heated a pot of hearty vegetable soup and cut off a few chunks of Otto's homemade bread to go with it for an early tea. After she'd eaten, she would dress warmly and go enjoy the fireworks. Hopefully, if Otto wasn't too late, he would be able to join her there.

As far as Dulcie was concerned, Bonfire Night drew a line under autumn and ushered in winter. She loved everything about it – the leaves underfoot (but only if they were dry and crunchy), the smell of woodsmoke, the aroma of sausages and onions (because Bonfire Night wasn't the same without a hotdog), and the heat from the fire itself. But most of all, she loved the way the fireworks lit up the heavens, those fleeting bursts of magical colours in the inky black sky. Even the loud bangs were fun: although Petra didn't agree, and Dulcie hoped the horses wouldn't be too spooked. Dulcie had left a radio playing in the barn so the goats and Flossie wouldn't get too stressed, and she had also popped another into the chicken coop.

It was totally dark when she parked the car on the edge of the village and made her way to where the display was being held. She had considered walking, and if Otto had been with her they may well have done, but she didn't fancy trekking across the fields on her own in the dark, so car it was. Anyway, Otto would probably just want to get home after all that travelling and the excitement of the day, and not have a half hour walk at the end of it.

Perhaps they could go out to celebrate tomorrow? Nothing fancy, just a drink in The Black Horse and maybe a takeaway. Then, if the time was right and she felt courageous enough, she would suggest he moved in with her.

Her tummy somersaulted at the thought. What if he said no? What if he hated the idea?

Or... maybe he would think it a fabulous idea and she would have worried for no reason, she countered, as she strode towards the park.

Argh! She hated being so dithery and nervous, but it was because she loved him so very much that she felt this way. It was a big deal to put herself out there and ask him to come live with her, and she felt justified for being worried. If he wasn't ready for such a commitment, she might spoil what they had, and that would be awful.

Putting her worries to one side, she scanned the crowd near the entrance to the park and quickly spotted her sister.

Hurrying over to her, Dulcie gave her a hug, then bent to hug Sammy. 'Gosh, I swear you've grown since I saw you last. Hi, Gio.' She waved at Nikki's partner. 'Who wants a sparkler?' she cried, spotting a man selling them.

'Me! Me!' Sammy jigged on the spot, and she was pleased to see his smiling face. Back in the summer he had been so miserable it had broken her heart. But a move to a new area and a new school, away from the bully who had made his life hell, and Sammy was a different child.

After a quick catch-up whilst Dulcie played with her sparkler – drawing her name in the air, obviously – the four of them made their way towards a cordoned-off area, ready to watch the display.

Dulcie checked her phone to see if there were any new messages from Otto, but there weren't, and her heart sank. Watching Nikki and Gio being so loved-up made her feel Otto's absence more keenly than she might otherwise have done if it had just been her and her sister. But everywhere she looked there were couples holding hands or snuggled into one another to keep warm.

'What time train was he catching?' Nikki asked, slipping her arm through Dulcie's.

'Not sure. Walter said he was meeting Alistair, his old boss at The Fern, for lunch.'

'Lucky thing! I wouldn't mind a spot of lunch out. But what with Sammy's football and judo – did I tell you he's joined the class in the community centre in Thornbury? – and Gio's awful shifts, we've hardly been out together at all since I moved to Picklewick. I'm either working myself, ferrying Sammy around, or Gio is at work. You're lucky having Otto there all the time.'

'We don't go out to lunch either,' Dulcie said.

'That's only because Otto prefers eating his own cooking,' Nikki pointed out.

Her sister was right (not about the cooking part, although Dulcie was very appreciative that her boyfriend loved to cook): she was lucky to have Otto around as much as he was. He was always there when she wanted him to be, which was more-or-less all the time. It was Dulcie herself whose time was limited because of her job. She envied couples who worked together; she could just imagine spending all day every day with Otto...

Music began to play and a flash lit up the sky as the firework display kicked off. For the next fifteen wonderful minutes Dulcie stood there with her face uplifted as she lost herself in the show. Only when the last sparks fizzled out did she check her phone again.

Her squeal of delight made Nikki jump.

'What's wrong?' her sister asked, concern in her eyes.

'Nothing's wrong, everything's **fine**! Otto is back. He's by the hotdog stand, so I think we ought to join him and treat ourselves to a snack at the same time.'

But little was she to know that everything was far from fine, and that things were very wrong indeed.

Otto had already decided not to tell Dulcie about Alistair's extraordinary and very tempting offer until he had made up his mind whether to accept it or not. Having three kitchens under his management, not to mention being given free rein to create mouthwatering and unusual recipes, was a dream come true.

Then there was the cherry on the top...

A restaurant dedicated to serving foraged and in-season foods that he would be in charge of, blew his mind. With this pedigree behind him, it would make finding a publisher far easier, and hopefully the book would fly off the shelves.

When Alistair had made the offer, Otto had been too shocked to respond for a moment, but after the news had sunk in, his first instinct had been to bite Alistair's hand off. And he almost had. Then Dulcie's face had swum into his mind, and he knew he had some serious thinking to do.

Telling Alistair that he needed some time and promising to get back to him early next week with an answer (Alistair understandably wanted to get the ball rolling on his new venture as soon as possible), Otto had thought about nothing else all the way home.

And that was the problem – that one little word. **Home.**

He hadn't considered Picklewick his home for many years, although he still referred to the farm as home. But the farm didn't belong to his dad anymore, it belonged to Dulcie. It was **her** home, not his. So where was home now?

In a kitchen, that's where. But at the moment he was homeless...

But Alistair had offered him not one home, but three! Four, if he counted the apartment his old boss was willing to throw in. Alistair was making it as easy as possible for Otto to say yes to the deal. And how could he forget that remarkable salary.

Alistair had gone on to outline his vision for each of the restaurants, and Otto's heart had leapt, before quickly sinking again.

If it hadn't been for Dulcie...

He sighed.

'What's up? I thought you would be bouncing with joy,' Dulcie said.

Otto blinked, then mentally shook his head to clear it. The woman he was madly in love with lifted her face to be kissed, and he swept her into his arms and lost himself in her embrace for several wonderful seconds.

Until Gio said, 'Get a room, you two,' and they broke apart sheepishly.

'Sorry,' Dulcie said, not looking in the slightest bit contrite. She looked like the cat who had stolen the cream, and Otto bit his lip as she said, 'Let's grab a hotdog and watch the bonfire being lit.'

'You go ahead. I'm not hungry.'

'Some of us didn't get to eat a Michelin star meal today,' she teased.

'Er...no. Sorry about that.' His dad must have told her he had lunched with Alistair, and he winced.

'No need to be. What did you have? Was it as good as when you were there? Better?' she joked.

'Um, I can't remember.' He knew he had eaten something, but he couldn't for the life of him remember what.

'You can't **remember**?' Dulcie was incredulous, then her gaze sharpened. 'What's wrong?' she asked.

'I'm tired, that's all. It's been a long day.'

He could tell from her expression that she didn't believe him, but thankfully Sammy tugged on her arm and she let it go.

But as soon as they were on their own, heading to the outskirts of the village to pick up Dulcie's little car, she began quizzing him about the meeting with Yvette.

'Tell me all about it,' she demanded. 'I was thinking about you all day, and when you messaged me to say she'd offered you a contract...!' She grabbed his upper arm and squeezed. 'That was the best news ever! When does she think she'll get a publisher for it? Did she say?'

'Not really,' he replied, and he went on to tell her what Yvette had told him.

'Oh, that's a bummer,' Dulcie commiserated, when he finished. 'I know how much you were depending on this. What will you do?'

He shrugged. 'Start looking for a job, I suppose.'

'In Thornbury?'

'If there is anything suitable available.'

They reached the car and Dulcie let go of him. She opened the driver's door. 'You don't think there will be?'

'I've looked previously, but you never know. Something might turn up.' Something had, but it hadn't been what he was expecting and it was miles away from Picklewick. The question was, if he were to take it, would Dulcie come with him?

There was only one thing for it – he had to find out.

'Can't get to sleep?' Dulcie rolled over and looked at the clock on the bedside table in concern. It was one thirty-three.

'I thought you were tired.' It had seemed that way, because when they had made love earlier, it hadn't been with their usual passion.

'Sorry, I'm keeping you awake. I'll go back to the cottage.'

'Please don't.' She turned to face him and propped herself up on an elbow. Otto's face was a pale disk in the darkness, the only light being a faint one from the clock. She wished she could make out his expression, because she had a feeling something was bothering him. 'What aren't you telling me? Is it to do with the book?'

'No. It is what it is. I just wish I'd known more about the process before I threw myself headlong into it.'

'What then? Are you worried about finding a job? Don't be: a chef with your skill will find one easily.'

She had every faith in him, even if he didn't have much in himself. Mind you, she conceded, it did depend on what jobs were out there, so he might have to apply for roles that were beneath head chef just to earn some money until a position he really wanted came along.

She did feel for him, though. It must have been hard giving up a prestigious position in a top London restaurant.

'I'm probably going to have to look further afield than Thornbury,' he told her.

Dulcie froze. 'How far?'

There was a timbre to his voice that she mightn't have picked up if it hadn't been for the darkness, and she sensed a tension in him that she hadn't noticed before tonight. She had a feeling there was something he wasn't telling her.

'Quite a bit further.' He shifted position so he was facing her.

'London,' she stated flatly, and suddenly everything was clear. He had been offered his old job back, and that was what the meeting with Alistair was about. Otto was moving back to London and was trying to find a way of letting her down gently.

'Um, maybe,' he said.

Before he could utter another word Dulcie sat up and swung her legs out of the bed, searching blindly for her slippers, tears close to the surface.

'Where are you going? We need to talk,' he said, his fingers brushing her hip as she stood up.

Hastily, she lifted her dressing gown off the hook on the back of the door and hurried out of the room. She could hear him coming after her as she headed for the stairs. Tears pricked her eyes, threatening to spill over, and she had a lump in her throat.

'Dulcie!' he called, pounding across the landing.

Otto caught her at the top of the stairs and gathered her to him. 'It's not what you think,' he began. 'Alistair—'

'Has offered you your old job back,' she finished, the tears welling over and trickling down her face.

'No, better than that. He's bought two more restaurants and wants me to run all three kitchens.'

He sounded more excited than she had ever heard him sound, and her heart turned to ice. **She had lost him.**

Too upset to speak, she backed away, moving out of his embrace, waiting for him to tell her it was over.

But what he said next, shocked her even more.

'I want you to come to London with me. Alistair has thrown in a flat as part of the deal, so we'll have somewhere to live, and you can work from anywhere, so you don't have to give up your job if you don't want to.'

She couldn't think straight. The only thing she could focus on was that he had asked her to go with him. He wasn't dumping her after all.

It was worse than that.

He wanted her to leave Picklewick; leave the new life she had embraced wholeheartedly; leave the farm she had fallen in love with and had big dreams for. Leave all this behind so he could follow his own dreams...

Could she do that? Give all this up to move to a city where she knew no one, apart from Otto?

Perhaps... But there was one thing preventing her from saying yes. 'If I say no, will you go back to London anyway?'

His hesitation told her everything she needed to know.

Dulcie had read somewhere that true love was being able to let go, to release the person you love, to set them free. And that was what she would have to do.

Otto loved her, she didn't doubt that. And she loved him, totally and utterly. Which was why she was about to let him go, to set him free to follow his dream.

It would break her heart when he left – hell, it was broken already – but that momentary pause when she asked him whether he would stay, made her mind up, despite his protests that of course he wouldn't leave if she wouldn't go with him. She could hear in his voice and see in his eyes how badly he wanted this. The half-moon shining through the landing window and illuminating the hope on his face, showed her just **how much** he wanted it.

She wished she had closed the curtains, so the darkness hid his face the way it had done in her bedroom, but even if she had, she still would have heard the hunger in his voice.

There was no way she could live with herself if she stopped him from doing what he loved.

He mightn't have said it out loud, but that brief hesitation had told her that although he loved her, he didn't love her **enough**. It had entered his head that he would go whether she went with him or not, and that is why she had to end it now.

Was she being hypocritical in that she had also hesitated when he had asked her to leave Picklewick? Could he also apply the same reasoning to her?

Probably. Definitely...

Maybe **he** could accuse **her** of not loving him enough...

But she could see no way to make this work. He wanted to live in London. She didn't. Despite having lived in a big city all her life, she had become a country girl through and through. She would suffocate in London — when she had told Carla that she didn't miss the noise, the crowds, the traffic... she had meant it. The farm on Muddypuddle Lane had wormed its way under her skin and deep into her heart, and she loved living here. She didn't think she would be able to adjust to being in a city again.

Then there was Otto's job itself... Long, unsociable hours. No worse than for anyone else who worked shifts, she acknowledged, but without the farm to occupy her what would she do with all that time on her own? There was only so much shopping or going to the gym a girl could do.

Would she and Otto go the same way as Remi and Steff?

They would tell themselves they would make it work, and maybe they could, but she knew she would eventually grow to resent him taking her away from Picklewick.

But god, this **hurt**.

'Speak to me,' he urged. 'Say something.' He was waiting for her response to his insistence that he wouldn't go unless she went with him.

'I think you should take the job,' she said. His face lit up, but when she added, 'I won't be coming with you,' his expression crumpled.

Please don't cry, she urged silently. She didn't think she could stand it if he did. As it was, she was on the cusp of giving in and telling him she would follow him to the ends of the earth: if he broke down, she was positive she would make a decision she would regret later.

Set him free, let him fly, she reminded herself.

'This job is everything you've ever wanted. You **have** to take it. You owe it to yourself,' she said. 'You would be a fool to turn it down.'

'Nuh-uh.' He was shaking his head. 'I'm not going without you. If you don't want to move to London, I'll stay here. Something tasty is bound to turn up.'

'It won't be as tasty as this,' she pointed out, and she saw by the look on his face that he agreed with her, although he tried to hide it.

She took a deep breath and willed herself to stay strong. She was doing this for **him**, because she loved him, as she said, 'You may as well take it. I wasn't going to say anything tonight, but you've kind of forced my hand – I don't think we're right for each other. We've had a lot of fun, but...'

She left the rest of the sentence hanging. Not because she was being deliberately cruel, but because she didn't think she could hold herself together for much longer.

'You can't mean that?' The disbelief in his voice was evident. 'Please say you don't mean that.'

Dulcie cleared her throat, despair washing over her. 'I do.'

He was staring at her and the hurt in his eyes was too much to bear. So she stood to the side, and dropped her gaze to the floor, hoping her intention was clear: that she wanted him to leave.

But when he moved past her, she saw the glint of tears in his eyes and she almost relented.

It's for the best, she told herself.

The best for **him**, not for **her**.

Because she had just let the only man she would ever love walk out of her door and out of her life, and she didn't know how she was supposed to carry on without him.

Don't cry, don't cry. As a mantra, it sucked, but thinking those four words over and over was better than thinking about all the other words that Dulcie had said tonight. Otto still couldn't take them in, especially the ones telling him that she didn't think they were right for each other. He refused to believe it. They were **perfect** for each other, and she knew it.

So how was it possible for her to have fallen out of love with him so quickly?

Or had she been leading him on when she had told him she loved him?

That was the more likely explanation... she hadn't loved him at all.

The pain in his heart was unbearable, and he didn't know what to do with himself. He didn't want to go to the cottage in case he woke Walter, because his dad would ask questions Otto didn't want to answer. He would have to tell his father soon that he and Dulcie had split up, but not tonight. There would be time enough tomorrow. The old man would be devastated. He thought the world of Dulcie.

He would also tell him about Alistair's offer, but he wasn't sure whether his father would encourage him to take it or not.

Otto headed up the hill, away from the cottage and the farm, aiming for the open moorland above. He needed to try to come to terms with what had happened, but he guessed it would take more than a walk in the fresh air to grasp the reality that he and Dulcie were over.

And all because of that damned offer.

If he hadn't told her about it, they would still be together.

Or would they?

Had she meant it when she had said they weren't right for each other anyway?

Gah, he was going over and over it in his head, his thoughts circling like water down the plughole. An endless supply of 'what if', and 'did she mean it'. He was going over the same ground again and again, and getting nowhere.

But he still wished he hadn't told her about the job.

He'd had to though, because how else would he have known whether she would have gone with him?

Although, if she was telling the truth (and why wouldn't she be?) Alistair's job had nothing to do with her decision to end their relationship, but he couldn't shift the suspicion that it did.

At least it made his decision easier. He could take the blasted job if he only had himself to please. His dad would understand – he knew that Otto lived for cooking. It was the opportunity of a lifetime and, as Dulcie rightly said, he would be a fool to turn it down.

He would have turned it down for her, though. Dulcie meant more to him than any job, no matter how sweet. He would have stayed in Picklewick and—

Otto slapped a hand to his forehead.

The sneaky madam! The unselfish, wonderful, thoughtful **madam**!

He knew what she was playing at, and it wouldn't work. But he also knew how stubborn she could be when she got an idea in her head – so he would just have to play her at her own game and convince her that he didn't want the damned job in the first place.

And he would be telling the truth – because without Dulcie by his side, the job was meaningless.

CHAPTER NINE

From her bedroom window Dulcie could just about see the chimney belonging to the cottage on Muddypuddle Lane. Although she couldn't see anything other than that of Walter's house, she didn't seem able to prevent herself from traipsing up the stairs every so often to peer through the glass.

She had been doing it all weekend, in a vain attempt to feel closer to Otto, but it was now Monday afternoon and she hadn't caught a single glimpse of him. Neither had there been any contact from him, although why she should expect any after telling him they were over was beyond her. Except... a part of her (the unreasonable part) wanted to think that he would have at least tried to fight for her. But then again, she reasoned, why fight for someone when they didn't love you as much as you hoped? He probably thought he was on a hiding to nothing, and he would be even more hurt than he was already.

Dulcie was about to turn away from the window and go do what she was paid to do, when she heard the rumble of an engine.

Her heart leapt and began to race, but it dropped like a stone to her boots when she saw Nikki's little hatchback turn into the farmyard.

She met her sister in the hall. 'Did you see Otto's car at the cottage?' she demanded before Nikki had a chance to say anything.

Her sister pursed her lips. 'No, sorry, it wasn't there.'

Dulcie felt like crying. Sick and heartbroken, she wondered whether Otto had left for London already.

'Have you eaten anything today?' Nikki asked, pushing past her and striding through the dining room and into the kitchen. 'I bet you haven't,' she said, as Dulcie followed behind. 'Let me make you something. You've got to eat.'

'I'm not hungry.'

'That's beside the point. You'll be ill if you don't. How about an omelette, or cheese on toast? Or you could come to mine for tea? We're having tuna pasta.'

Dulcie shuddered. The mention of food made her think of Otto, and her stomach churned. 'Do you think he's left yet?' she said.

'Dulcie...' Nikki warned. 'You've got to eat.'

'I'll have something later.'

'You'll have it **now**. I'm making you an omelette and you'd better eat it.' She began rummaging in the fridge.

Dulcie ignored her. 'Do you think I should check on Walter? He's bound to be upset, especially if Otto has left already.'

'He might not have done,' Nikki said. 'Just because his car's not there...'

'Who's looking after Sammy?' Dulcie asked, suddenly realising that Nikki must have driven straight to the farm as soon as she'd finished work.

'He's at an after-school club. I'm picking him up in an hour. I wanted to check you were okay first.'

Dulcie was not okay; she didn't think she'd be okay for a very long time indeed. 'Don't worry about me, I'm fine.'

'You aren't,' Nikki retorted, cracking three eggs into a bowl, whisking them vigorously, then pouring the mixture into a hot pan. 'Aside from the puffy eyes and the dark circles, I know you inside and out Dulcie Fairfax... and you're far from fine. And no, I don't think you should go see Walter – Otto might be there.' Nikki sent her a keen look. 'Or have you changed your mind about moving to London with him?'

'It's too late for that. Even if I have, I've blown it.'

'So, **have** you changed it?'

'It's all I've been able to think about. What if I've made the biggest mistake of my life?'

'Then it's up to you to try to unmake it.'

'What if I **can't**?'

'What if you **can**?' Nikki countered. 'Here, eat this.' She slid the omelette onto a plate and placed it in front of her.

The smell made Dulcie feel nauseous, but she knew she had to eat, and Nikki had gone to all that trouble to make her the food. With a distinct lack of enthusiasm, she picked up a fork and broke a small piece off. It was similar to how she imagined dry chicken pellets might taste,

but she ploughed through it, Nikki
hovering over her.

'I can't eat any more,' she said finally,
pushing the remains of the half-eaten
omelette away.

'Hmm.' Nikki inspected it. 'I suppose it's
better than nothing. I've got to go – I
need to pick Sammy up. Try to get some
sleep tonight, yeah?'

'If you see Otto's car outside the cottage,
will you message me?'

'I will,' Nikki promised. She gave Dulcie a
hug.

Dulcie watched her leave, then went back
to work. But her mind wasn't on her job.
How could it be, when she had lost the
love of her life through her own stupidity
and selfishness?

Otto threw his car keys onto the mantelpiece and slumped into a chair, exhausted. These past couple of days had been a whirlwind of activity.

'Well?' Walter demanded.

'They've got to run a few financial checks and obtain references, but it's looking good.'

He rubbed a weary hand across his face. He was so tired that he didn't know what to do with himself. That was what comes of being unable to sleep for three nights, he thought. But even if he hadn't had this madcap idea, he wouldn't have been able to sleep. Being heartbroken wasn't the best recipe for restful slumber. Add to that the thoughts swirling around his head at a hundred miles an hour, and he was unlikely to get much sleep tonight either.

'Are you sure this is what you want to do?' his dad asked.

'I'm sure.' Otto had never been more sure of anything in his life – aside from his love for Dulcie. He just hoped this wasn't in vain.

His dad voiced Otto's fear. 'What if she meant it when she said you two aren't right for each other?'

'I refuse to believe it. As I said, she's doing what she thinks is right for me. But what is right for me, is **Dulcie**.'

'Have you told Alistair of your decision?'

'Not yet. I'd better phone him now.' Otto heaved himself to his feet. This wasn't a conversation he was looking forward to.

He hated letting his old boss down, but if he was to have any chance of winning Dulcie back, he had no choice.

'Alistair? It's Otto,' he said, when his former boss answered. 'I'm sorry but I won't be taking you up on your incredibly generous offer. It's a fantastic job for someone… just not for me. You see, Dulcie doesn't want to move to London and I'm not prepared to move without her. I'm staying here. I intend to open a restaurant in Picklewick instead.'

Sod it, I've not got anything to lose, Dulcie thought. She couldn't face one more minute of this indecision. Five days was long enough. It was time to make her mind up one way or the other. She either had to let Otto go, or she had to tell him the truth about her feelings for him.

If he hadn't already gone...

Shoving her feet into her wellies, Dulcie stuffed her arms into her padded jacket and zipped it up, then grabbed a box of eggs. She would use it as an excuse to knock on Walter's door.

Ignoring the hopeful bleats from the barn (she had already fed the goats and Flossie), Dulcie trotted across the farmyard and down the lane, praying she wasn't too late. If Otto would just give her a chance to explain why she'd said what she had said, that was all she hoped.

She still didn't want to relocate to London, but being there with him was infinitely better than being here **without** him. She would soon get used to living in a city again; she had done it once so she could do it again. And in no time at all, she would look back on her time at the farm as nothing more than an extended holiday... although she would find it hard to see a stranger living there. Just as Otto had found it hard to see her occupying the house he had grown up in. He'd got used to it, though, and so would she.

To her immense disappointment, Otto's car wasn't parked in its usual spot outside the cottage, and she tried not to panic that she was too late. He could be anywhere: shopping, getting his hair cut, having his car serviced... **anywhere**.

But when she knocked on the door there was no answer, and after waiting a moment and knocking a second time with the same lack of response, she assumed that Walter wasn't in either.

The sound of an engine coming up the lane made her freeze, hope surging through her, but when she saw it was Petra's Land Rover, she sagged with disappointment. Amos was at the wheel, and she suddenly realised that she hadn't seen either man since she and Otto had split up. Work had stalled on the goats' shelter, and she guessed she was the reason. She didn't blame Walter for not wanting to help – why should he?

She supposed she would have to try to complete it herself. Walter must hate her for hurting his son; **if,** in fact, Otto was hurting as much as she. He might not be – he might be so caught up in this new job of his that he hadn't given her a second thought.

Still, she couldn't get the look on his face out of her head when she'd told him they were over. He had looked broken.

Which was exactly how she felt.

She hadn't realised how much a broken heart could hurt, or how deep the pain.

Seeing Amos, Dulcie leapt at the opportunity to pick his brains, and she flagged him down. 'Do you know if Walter is okay? I can't get any answer.' She would hate for him to have a relapse.

'I saw him yesterday and he was fine. Sorry to hear about you and Otto.'

Not as sorry as Dulcie was – and it was all her own fault. She hated herself for asking, but she simply had to know. 'Has Otto gone back to London yet?'

Amos blinked. 'I didn't know he **was** going back. I thought—'

The door to the cottage opened abruptly, and Walter cried, 'Dulcie! I thought there was someone at the door. How lovely!'

Dulcie turned around to see him on his doorstep. He beckoned her closer.

'I've brought you some eggs,' she said, handing them to him. 'And I wanted to see how you are coping now that Otto has gone back to London.'

'He hasn't left yet. There's no rush,' Walter said. He didn't sound as upset as she thought he would be, and she was glad. He also knew that Otto's heart lay elsewhere, and he had accepted it a long time ago. She knew how incredibly proud he was of his son, and she also knew that he wouldn't want to hold him back from what he loved doing.

Neither did she... which was why she was here.

'Shall I tell him you called?' Walter asked.

Dulcie bit her lip. 'Yes, please.'

'I would ask you in, but I don't know when he'll be back. He's...er...got a bit of business to attend to, and I was in the middle of...' He trailed off.

'It's okay.' She fully appreciated how awkward this must be for him, but at least he was still speaking to her – she wouldn't have blamed him if he hadn't been. After all, she had dumped his son.

Feeling defeated, she gave him a sad little smile as she said goodbye, and went home.

She would just have to try to catch Otto later.

'Have you signed on the dotted line?' Walter asked as soon as Otto switched the engine off and got out of the car. His dad had been peering through the living room window and had hurried out to greet him.

'Give me a chance,' Otto said, smiling. 'Can we go inside first?'

'Dulcie was here earlier.'

Otto froze. 'What did she want?'

'She gave me some eggs, but I don't think that was the real reason. I wasn't going to answer the door because I was worried that I might give the game away, but by sheer bad luck Amos came up the lane at that very moment. I had to head him off at the pass, before he said something he shouldn't.'

'Did she suspect anything?'

'I don't think so, but you can't afford to hang about. Word will soon get around that you've taken the lease out on the old bric-a-brac shop, and she'll get to hear about it before long.'

'I want her to hear it from me first,' Otto said. He would have told her sooner, but he had been waiting for the contract to be signed and to have the keys in his hand. Should he go up to the farm and tell her now?

Suddenly his eyes widened. He had an idea!

'How do you feel about a bit of subterfuge?' Otto asked his father. 'It's in a good cause...'

Dulcie had trotted halfway down the lane a couple of times since speaking to Walter earlier in the day, in the hope of seeing Otto's car outside the cottage, but to no avail. He was still out.

Business, Walter had said, and as she popped a couple of slices of bread into the toaster, she wondered what kind of business.

Her appetite was still poor and she still didn't feel like eating, but after Nikki had practically force-fed food down her neck, Dulcie had promised her sister that she would take better care of herself and would eat a substantial meal each evening. Hoping beans on toast counted, she took a tin out of the cupboard, but before she could open it, her phone rang.

'Walter? Is everything okay?'

'Um, not really. I'm in a bit of a pickle. I hate to ask, but Otto isn't back yet, so...'

'Ask what? What do you need?'

'Can you take me to the chemist? I forgot to get my prescription filled and if I don't take my tablets...' He left another sentence hanging, and a shiver of alarm travelled down Dulcie's spine.

Walter didn't sound good. He sounded more like the frail old man she had met when she had first moved to Picklewick, and she prayed he wasn't having a relapse. He had been doing so well; just this morning he had looked hale and hearty, but now he sounded ill and old.

And there was something else that worried her. 'Walter,' she said gently, 'it's half-past six. The chemist won't be open.'

'It will. They don't shut until seven tonight. It's to do with the doctor's surgery having evening appointments.'

'Ah, I see. I'll be there in five minutes.'

Her concern that he was starting to become confused was alleviated by knowing that the chemist was open late, but as she set off down the lane, she continued to worry how he would cope without Otto around.

Walter didn't look as bad as she feared, she saw with relief, as she jumped out of the car and raced to open the passenger door for him. He had been waiting on the step, and he got in with a groan.

She asked, 'Are you okay?'

'Aye, can't grumble. Thanks for this, Dulcie. I really appreciate it.'

'Have you got your prescription?'

He smiled and patted his jacket pocket. 'I'm not senile yet.'

'I didn't say you were.'

They reached the end of Muddypuddle Lane, and she checked for oncoming traffic, then pulled out onto the road. It was a two-minute drive from here to get to the middle of the high street at this time of the evening, so she resisted the urge to put her foot down. As long as Walter made it to the chemist before they closed, they would hardly turn him away, even if it did take a few minutes to fill the prescription.

'Stop here!' Walter commanded, and Dulcie pulled into the kerb without thinking, before realising that the chemist was at the far end of the street.

'Um,' she began, but the old man was already getting out.

She leant across the passenger seat. 'Walter, it's not here, it's down there.' She pointed down the street.

'I think you'll find it **is** here,' he said, and he shut the car door firmly.

Worriedly, she scrambled out after him. 'Walter!'

Oh, dear, he was heading for an empty shop and trying the handle.

'Walter! That's not the chem—' Dulcie stopped.

The empty shop wasn't as empty as she first thought. There was a table in the middle of it, surrounded by lit candles on the floor, and a man standing next to it.

'Otto?' Confused, she turned to Walter. He was smirking.

'Thanks, Dad,' Otto said.

'Shall I wait up?'

Otto rolled his eyes. 'Just go.'

'Good luck, son. See you later, Dulcie. Much later, I hope.' And with that the old man was gone, the door shutting behind him with a click.

Silence reigned for a moment. Dulcie was too shocked and confused to speak, and Otto seemed at a loss for words.

Eventually he asked, 'Are you hungry?'

Mutely, she shook her head.

'Me, neither. Never mind, the food will keep.'

Dulcie found her voice. 'What food? What's going on, Otto?'

'I've got wine, if you fancy a glass.'

She thought she'd better had – a drink might help with the thudding in her chest and the pulse throbbing at her temple.

He popped the cork on a bottle of red, and poured the rich dark liquid into two crystal glasses which were sitting on the table. The table itself was covered by a white cloth and laid with cutlery.

He held one of the glasses out to her and she stepped closer to take it from him.

'What's going on?' she repeated. 'Why is there a table and candles? I don't understand.'

'Welcome to The Wild Side,' he said.

Dulcie stared blankly at him. Was Walter's confusion contagious? 'I was supposed to be taking your dad to get his prescription filled.'

'Yeah, sorry about the subterfuge, but I had to get you down here somehow.'

'Why?'

'Can I ask you a question first? Please? Then I'll tell you everything.'

'Okaaay.'

'Did you mean it when you said you don't think we are right for each other?'

Dulcie caught her bottom lip between her teeth, hesitated, then muttered, 'No.'

'So why did you say it?'

'That's two questions.'

'Humour me?'

'Because you wouldn't have taken the job otherwise.' She might as well be honest with him – she had planned to beg him to take her back, to take her to London with him, so...

He let out a long slow breath. 'I thought as much.'

'You did?'

'I'm not taking it.'

Dulcie frowned. 'But, I thought—'

'That it's my dream job?' he interrupted.

She nodded.

'It is, but I have another dream which means far more to me. I have a dream that we will marry and have kids, that we'll have a long and happy life, and that we will grow old together. And if that means staying in Picklewick, then I'll stay in Picklewick.'

Those were the most beautiful words she had ever heard. Gulping back tears, Dulcie said, 'You don't have to. I'll go to London with you. Heck, 'I'll go with you to the ends of the earth, if I have to. I'm so sorry I hurt you.'

He took the glass out of her hand and placed it on the table. '**I'm** not,' he said. 'It's made me realise what I truly want – and I want **you**.'

And with that he took her in his arms, his eyes so full of love it made her cry even harder, and he gently kissed her tears away. Then his mouth found hers and she clung to him so fiercely she thought she might never let him go.

'Why this elaborate set-up?' Dulcie asked later. They were sitting at the table laid for two and drinking the wine.

'Because I needed to convince you that I was serious about not taking the job with Alistair.'

'I don't follow. Why here? You could have just come to the farm and told me.'

'How was I to know you had changed your mind about coming with me to London? I believed you still thought you were stepping back so I would take the job.'

'Yes, but why **here**, in this old shop? If you didn't want to discuss it at the farm, you could have taken me to a restaurant and wined and dined...' She slowed to a halt as something he said earlier leapt into her mind. 'Is this what I **think** it is? Are you planning on opening your own restaurant?' Her voice rose an octave on the last word.

'I am. Do you mind?' Worry flitted across his face.

'Of course I don't mind! That's brilliant news.'

'It'll mean long hours setting it up, and equally long hours to establish a good reputation.'

'I don't care – you'll be doing what you love, what you were born to do.'

'But we won't see as much of each other as we're used to,' he said, regretfully. 'If I had my way I would spend every waking second with you.'

Dulcie giggled. 'Actually, I've been thinking about that. There is something I've been wanting to ask you, and it would mean that we would see each other every morning and every night. I'd like us to live together on the farm. What do you think?'

Otto looked stunned. His mouth dropped open and his eyes widened: then the biggest grin spread across his face. 'I think it is the best idea you had since buying that lottery ticket!'

And when Otto swept her into his arms again, she knew that the spark of love he had ignited in her heart all those months ago would never be extinguished.

There was no way the restaurant would be open in time for Christmas, Otto knew, but that didn't stop him from planning on working flat out to get it ready to open as soon as possible in the New Year.

'Are you sure you don't mind helping?' he asked Dulcie, for what was possibly the fifth time that morning. He thought she might have wanted to spend the weekend relaxing – she did work five days a week, and this last week had been pretty fraught – but she had thrown herself into the renovations with enthusiasm. Luckily the front of house area didn't need a great deal of work, not compared to what would eventually be the kitchen. Then there was the walk-in fridge to sort out, and customer toilets to install.

Otto guestimated that the work would take at least two months, and that's if there weren't any unforeseen delays, which he sincerely hoped there wouldn't as his budget was severely stretched as it was. He was having great fun designing the place though, and he had pulled together a list of things he liked about other restaurants, as well as the things he didn't, and he had made a mood board to work from.

Meanwhile, Dulcie was researching setting up a website with an online booking system, and he was very grateful for her help because it was the admin side of the restaurant business that had put him off opening his own in the first place.

He still wasn't sure he was doing the right thing, although he was seriously looking forward to getting back into a kitchen again.

It was while he was standing in what would eventually become the kitchen, and planning out where each piece of equipment would go, that he received the first of two important phone calls of the day.

Dulcie was stripping layers of old paint off the wall in the main part of the restaurant, but she downed tools so he could hear himself speak.

'Hi, Yvette.' He was surprised to hear from his agent, having practically forgotten about his cookbook in the events of the last two weeks.

Yvette said, 'I've got some brilliant news. At least three publishers are interested – I'll email you the details of the contracts on offer, and when you've had a chance to read through them, give me a call and we'll have a chat about it.'

'**Three?** Did I hear you correctly?'

'You did. I must admit, I wasn't expecting that, but word of your new restaurant has got out. Just wait until it gains a Michelin star of its own! Publishers will be falling over you to offer you a contract on the next book.'

'The next book,' he repeated woodenly. He doubted there would be a next one, and after the call ended, he said as much to Dulcie.

'Nonsense! If this sells as well as I believe it will, you'll **have** to write another. You can try the recipes out on your diners.'

The next call was just as surprising.

It was from Alistair.

Otto got in first. 'Do I have you to thank for spreading the word about The Wild Side?' he asked, after he had told Alistair his publishing news. The man knew more people than the devil, and most of them had dined in The Fern at some point.

'I may have whispered in an ear or two,' Alistair admitted. 'But that's not why I'm calling. I still want you to be my Menu Director.'

Otto's good mood dipped. What was Alistair playing at? 'You know I can't.'

'You **can**,' Alistair insisted. 'You can work out of your own kitchen, and I'll send my chefs to you to be trained. Once a month you can pop down to London to quality-assure the dishes. It's a win-win situation for both of us.'

'It'll be bloody hard work for me.'

'It'll be bloody **lucrative** for you,' Alistair countered. 'And it'll put your name and that of your restaurant firmly on the map.'

Otto looked at Dulcie.

She was beaming at him and holding both thumbs up. 'Go for it,' she mouthed. 'You'll regret it if you don't.'

He knew she was right.

So he said yes. Just as he hoped she would say yes when he asked her to marry him.

Not now, but soon... They had a restaurant to open first, and a farm to run.

Never had Otto been so busy, and never had he been as happy; and when Dulcie threw herself into his arms, demanding kisses, he vowed that no matter how busy or how frantic life became he would always, **always** put this wonderful woman first, because her love was the only thing that truly mattered.

There are loads more large print books in the Muddypuddle Lane series. Available at all good book stores, or ask your local library.

About Etti

Etti Summers is the author of wonderfully romantic fiction with happy ever afters guaranteed.

She is also a wife, a mum, a pink gin enthusiast, a veggie grower and a keen reader.